That Football Game

AND WHAT CAME OF IT

"To the spectators it seemed as though Harry Archer were carrying the opposing eleven on his back. He shook off one, then another."

That Football Game

AND WHAT CAME OF IT

By

Fr. Francis J. Finn, S.J.

AUTHOR OF TOM PLAYFAIR, PERCY WYNN,
HARRY DEE, ETC.

TAN BOOKS AND PUBLISHERS, INC.
Rockford, Illinois 61105

Copyright © 1893 by Benziger Brothers, Inc., New York.

Retypeset and published in 2003 by TAN Books and Publishers, Inc.

ISBN 0-89555-713-4

Library of Congress Control No.: 2001-132399

Cover illustration © 2002 by Phyllis Pollema-Cahill. Cover illustration rendered expressly for this book and used by arrangement with Wilkinson Studios, Chicago.

Cover design by Peter Massari, Rockford, Illinois.

Printed and bound in the United States of America.

TAN BOOKS AND PUBLISHERS, INC.
P.O. Box 424
Rockford, Illinois 61105
2003

"I regard football as the greatest of all games, principally for the reason that it schools a boy to almost heroic self-restraint both on and off the field."   —Pages 21-22

"Football is essentially a young gentlemen's game. It is quite feasible, at times, to play a game of baseball with rough characters; but in football, you must play only with gentlemen—otherwise the game becomes a slugging match and a question as to which is the better or worse set of rowdies."

—Page 25

CONTENTS

CHAPTER I

A Little Poetry, a Little of Mathematics, with the
Prospects of a Great Deal about Football   . . .   1

CHAPTER II

In which the Milwaukee College Eleven Begin to
Feel the Iron Hand of Discipline 16

CHAPTER III

In which It Is shown that the Game of Football,
with its Severe Preparatory Work, Has Many
Points in Its Favor 27

CHAPTER IV

The Home of Harry Archer 41

CHAPTER V

Showing How a Want of Ready Money Is Not
Always a Thing To Be Deplored 50

CHAPTER VI

In which Mathematicians Are Given their Due . . . 62

CHAPTER VII

In which It Is Shown that Football May Be a Help
both to Study and to Devotion 72

CHAPTER VIII
In which New Troubles Visit the Archer Family . . 81

CHAPTER IX
In which Harry Begins to Suspect that He Is
    Burning the Candle at Both Ends 95

CHAPTER X
In which Harry and Claude Take a Drive 118

CHAPTER XI
In which the Morning of Thanksgiving Day Reveals
    Serious Internal Dissensions in the Football
    Team 127

CHAPTER XII
In which Mr. Keenan Faces an Indignant Mother
    and Is More Frightened than He ever Was
    Since He Came to the Use of Reason 138

CHAPTER XIII
On the way to the Football Field 152

CHAPTER XIV
In which Mandolin Merry and Mary Dale Learn
    Something of the Great Game 159

CHAPTER XV
In which the Milwaukees Play the First Half
    under Great Difficulties 177

CHAPTER XVI
In which Ernest Snowden Surprises Everybody, and
    the Great Football Game Comes to an End . 211

CHAPTER XVII

In which Harry Learns that He Cannot Compete
in the Mathematical Contest 232

CHAPTER XVIII

In which It Is shown that Doctors May
Compare Favorably with even the Best
of Mathematicians 240

CHAPTER XIX

In which the Prospects for the Archer Family
Grow Brighter 249

CHAPTER XX

In which Everybody Is Happy and the Curtain
Falls 254

That Football Game

AND WHAT CAME OF IT

Chapter I

MR. GEORGE KEENAN, Professor of Poetry Class, having heard the recitation in Rhetoric and given a new lesson and an English theme for the following day, took up a bundle of papers from his desk.

There was a slight stir in the class indicative of awakening interest. Mr. Keenan had the gift of arousing enthusiasm in regard to English writing, and, in consequence, his scholars were ever ready to listen with eager interest to his comments on their attempts, whether in verse or in prose.

"I have examined this set of verses," began the professor, "with much interest and pleasure. Out of eighteen exercises, twelve are very creditable. For imagination, Claude Lightfoot's is far the best, while for finish of versification, Dan Dockery's is admirable. I shall read these presently and also three or four others—Stein's, Pearson's, O'Rourke's, and Desmond's. But business before pleasure.

I have here a set of verses which, while they would not be particularly discreditable to a student in Humanities, are not all that one expects from a member of Poetry class. Here we expect something more than verse and rhymes, which are merely the dry bones of poetry; every English exercise given you in this class, unless it is expressly stated otherwise, is supposed to have some touch of passion, in the rhetorical sense of that word. Now listen to this:

A POEM ON NIGHT

The sun has slowly gone to rest
Behind the mountains in the west.
It gets a good deal darker now,
The bird stops singing on the bough;
The stars come out and at us peep,
And little children go to sleep,
And chickens, too, go off to roost.

"By the way," interpolated Mr. Keenan, "are we to infer that children go to roost, too?"

And watchdogs from their chains are loosed,
The stars come out, the moon shines, too,
Although a cloud hides it from view.
The crickets chirp, the bullfrog croaks,
And many a man goes off and smokes.

The reading was here interrupted by an outbreak of laughs and giggles. Mr. Keenan held up his hand.

"Here, now," he said, "you have an example of how *not* to write poetry. The boy who composed this never for one moment during the composition of his doggerel placed before his imagination one concrete picture of night. He simply took nights in general and looked at them piecemeal. Hence, there is no order, no unity, no choice of details, nothing that would give an idea to the listener of any particular night from the beginning of Spring to the end of Autumn. The composer's imagination is as dry as a stick. I dare say he hasn't read three good books during the entire vacation just passed. Anyone reading these verses can see that in writing them he was 'most unusual calm.'"

Just as this point a hand went up. It was Harry Archer's.

"Well, Harry?" said Mr. Keenan, returning a smile for the grin on the student's face.

"I wasn't 'most unusual calm,' sir, when I wrote those verses."

"Ah, you have told on yourself, Harry," said Mr. Keenan, as several of the boys turned their merry eyes on Archer with new interest.

"Oh, they all know the way I write from last year, sir; and it doesn't matter, anyhow.

But so far from being 'most unusual calm,' I was almost tearing my hair out after I got to the seventh line in one hour, and stuck there for almost another, trying to get a rhyme for roost. By the time I loosed those dogs on the scene, I was so mad that I could have done something desperate."

Mr. Keenan laughed.

"Why, Harry, your own confession shows that you need not despair. Put your passion into your verse instead of pulling at your hair, and then who knows but you will turn out a poet."

Mr. Keenan was about to read Claude Lightfoot's verse on the same subject when the door of the classroom opened and Father Hogan, vice president of the college [academy], entered, followed by a young gentleman of sixteen.

The newcomer was attired in the extreme of fashion—his suit was of the lightest color, his trousers, below the knees, were of the widest; his hair was very long, parted in the middle, and plastered down on either side of the parting so as to allow only a small triangular portion of his forehead to be seen. For the rest, he was stout, cherry-cheeked, pretty and, aside from the evidence of scented handkerchief and many jewels, decidedly effeminate. The newcomer was smiling recognition to nearly everybody in the room. He kissed his hand to Claude Lightfoot.

"Mr. Keenan," said the vice president, "I bring you a new member for your class— Willie Hardy, who for the past two years has been attending classes as a boarder at St. Maure's College [Academy]."

"You are welcome," said Mr. Keenan, taking the boy's hand in his.

Willie Hardy advanced his right foot, drew back his left, and bowed so low that the professor was able to trace the parting of his hair as far as the nape of his neck, where, for obvious reasons, it ended.

"It is not necessary, Mr. Keenan," proceeded the vice president, "for me to introduce Willie Hardy to the students of this class. Willie has told me that he was with them in Second Academic, and I am sure they all remember him very well."

"I know *I* do," said Claude Lightfoot, with the sunny smile which he had carried undimmed up and on through the lower classes; whereat all the listeners, morally speaking, broke into a roar of laughter.

Mr. Keenan and the vice president were puzzled by this outburst of merriment. They were both unacquainted with Willie Hardy personally, and, luckily for that smiling youth, knew nothing of his record at Milwaukee College [Academy]; and, as Willie joined in with the laughing quite heartily, they were not moved to inquire further into the matter.

The vice president withdrew; Willie was assigned a seat next to Claude Lightfoot, and Mr. Keenan was about to resume class work when the bell rang for the end of class.

"By the way," said Mr. Keenan, "don't forget about the meeting in the gymnasium of the members of the football team."

Then he said prayers with the class and dismissed them. As Willie Hardy was going out, he motioned him to remain.

Willie stood smiling and radiant while the students marched out two by two into the corridor. One other boy, however, remained. It was Harry Archer. He was very red in the face, and very nervous.

"What's the matter, Harry?" inquired the professor kindly.

"I—I've come to tell you, sir, that I can't play football this year."

Mr. Keenan had considerable command over his feelings, but I am bound to say that at this announcement his jaw dropped.

"Why, Harry," he exclaimed, "you're not in earnest, are you? We can't get along without our quarterback."

"Oh, you will find plenty of good material, I hope, sir. I am awfully sorry, for I love the game, and I want to see Milwaukee College head and shoulders over every team in the city, but I can't play this year."

"I doubt very much," Mr. Keenan made answer, "whether we have plenty of good material; but even granting this, there is no one in the college—in fact I believe, from what I have heard—there is no one in the city who can at all compare with you as quarterback. Are you quite serious in your resolution?"

"Indeed, I am, Mr. Keenan. I have been thinking about the matter ever since the middle of last August; and since the opening of classes last week, I have been thinking of it harder than ever. The fact is, I have been trying to find some excuse to play, but I really can't. I am convinced that it is my duty to keep out of the game for this season."

"I think I could play quarterback," said Willie Hardy, who had been listening thus far with no attempt to conceal his interest.

"I hope, Harry," Mr. Keenan went on, taking no notice, under stress of his disappointment, of Willie—"I hope that my reading of your verses and my comments on them have had nothing to do with your decision."

"Oh indeed, no, Mr. Keenan!" protested Harry with much earnestness. "I know that my verses are bad, and the few words you said have convinced me that I ought to do a little reading, but I spend so much time at studying that I find none for books."

"How much time do you give to your studies?"

"From three to five hours, sir."

Here Willie, who was now standing behind Mr. Keenan, thrust his tongue into his cheek, and winked at Harry. The object of these polite attentions, however, failed to acknowledge the signals. Willie felt sure that Harry was lying and had thrown out these familiar signs to signify in the most friendly manner possible his opinion to that effect.

"Well," said Mr. Keenan, "I would advise you to throw off an hour from your studies and give it to reading."

"But, sir, I am working for that eighty-dollar prize for the best examination in Geometry."

"Even so, Harry, that work need not engross your time; as a mathematician you are far and away the best in the class. Claude Lightfoot, excellent as he is, can't come near you."

"Yes, but that's because I study at it three or four times as long as Claude. If I were to let down in my work, Claude would run away from me in Mathematics in a week."

"That may be so, Harry; but meantime you are giving so much time to Mathematics and so little to English that you are in danger of injuring your literary gifts. If you were to pay more attention to each, you would secure a much better mental development. Mathematics and literary studies correct each other. An excess of Mathematics narrows or even dries up the imagination, while an excess in the study of literature develops looseness, vagueness and inaccuracy. You must try to balance yourself."

"That is true, sir; but I have made up my mind to get that eighty-dollar prize, if it is possible; and in the meantime I must let literature, outside of regular class work, go. After Thanksgiving Day I hope that I shall be able to do better."

"I shall be delighted, Harry, if you secure the prize. It will be an honor to our class and to our college."

"A good many high-school boys and private students under eighteen are working for it, and some of them have hired special coaches."

"Is anyone helping you?"

"No, sir; I am working pretty much by

myself. Mr. Lawrence, who taught us Geometry in Humanities, gave me a splendid start, and I find that under you I am learning, if anything, faster than ever."

Here Willie Hardy interposed.

"I thay," he said with a pronounced lisp, "what ith thith thing all about? Whothe going to give a prithe of eighty dollarth?"

"Didn't you hear about it yet?" cried Archer. "Have you been away from Milwaukee this summer?"

"Yeth," said Willie sweetly; "I wath thpending my time out at a lake where there wath nobody to dithturb me. I gave nine hourth a day to reading poetry."

Mr. Keenan, who knew nothing of Willie, was impressed with this statement. Archer was impressed, too, but for a different reason. That richness of fancy which had made Willie notorious in former years at Milwaukee College had not deserted the pretty youth. He still lied with elegance and ease.

"Well, Willie," said the professor, "on the tenth of August last, the *Evening Wisconsin* offered a prize of eighty dollars to any boy or girl under the age of nineteen who should make the best examination in Geometry. It is open to any young person in Milwaukee who, on the thirtieth of November next, shall present himself or herself at the Public Library Reading Room with one hundred coupons cut out from the issues of the *Evening Wisconsin.* Those who are to compete must come to the reading room with no paper of any kind save the one hundred coupons, which are to serve as tickets of admission. Paper, pens and ink are to be provided by the proprietors of the paper. Sharp at nine o'clock on the morning of November the thirtieth, every competitor will be handed a slip containing some fifteen or twenty propositions and problems in Geometry. These propositions and problems are to be made out by the city editor of the *Wisconsin,* who is an able mathematician; and as he is one of the projectors of the enterprise and a man of the most scrupulous honor, you see that there is little or no danger of unfairness. Now, Harry," continued Mr. Keenan, turning his eyes upon the young mathematician, "I think I see a chance to get you some extra help. How would you like to have a coach who would do his work for you as a labor of love?"

Harry's eyes danced.

"Oh! I should be infinitely obliged to you," he said.

"I should be glad to coach you myself, were

it not for two reasons. First, I have to give most of my time, outside of class work and preparation for it, to keeping athletics going among the boys. (This, it may be said in parenthesis, was quite true.) Secondly, even if I were free, I don't think that I should be of any assistance to you, as I am but a poor mathematician."

In giving the second reason, Mr. Keenan allowed his modesty to get the better of his judgment.

"I wouldn't think of letting you help me, sir," put in Harry, "because I know you have more than enough to do."

"Not more than enough, Harry. We never have too much to do, so long as we love our work and are able to do it. But there is a young Father in the college who has given all his free time for the last ten years to mathematics. He is now engaged in writing a book on Calculus and some time ago offered to help me in any way he could. I think that if I mention your case to him he will gladly give you a few hours a week. I have met many mathematicians, but no one who at all approaches him. If he finds that you have the ability, he will give you a training such as no boy in Milwaukee is likely to get."

"My!" cried Archer, "wouldn't that be fine!"

"There wath a profether at Thaint Maureth who could square the thircle," put in Willie.

Taking no notice of the remark, Mr. Keenan went on.

"Now, Harry, in case I get Father Trainer to help you, I want you to promise in return that once the contest is over, you will give yourself with energy—and I know you have plenty of it—to your English."

"I promise right here and now, Mr. Keenan; and honestly, I feel as though you were heaping coals of fire upon my head. Here I come and disappoint you very much, as I can see, by refusing to play in the college eleven; and in return, you try to help me as though I were your best friend. Oh! I should like to play; it makes me feel so mean to refuse; but I can't, sir. One reason is that I wish to give extra time to study, but that's only a small part. I should like to tell you the other reason, but I can't do it yet. Later on, sir, I hope to be able to tell you."

"Very good, Harry. I am convinced that you are acting under a sense of duty; and, while I am sorry to lose you, I would rather have no eleven at all than have a single boy on it who was playing to the detriment of higher and more important interests."

"Thank you, Mr. Keenan. I hope to be able to do something for you and for the college in the way of athletics next Spring. Good afternoon, sir."

"Good afternoon, Harry; and be careful, my boy, not to study too much. Keep your health and strength. Even during these first ten or twelve days of class, I have noticed that your color is not so good as it was when I first met you last August, and there is the least little sign of a black circle under your eyes."

"Oh, I'm pretty strong, sir; but I'll try to look out."

"Now, Willie," said Mr. Keenan, as Harry left the room, "perhaps you can be of some use to me. Are you a football player?"

"That ith my favorite game."

"Were you on the first eleven of St. Maure's?"

"No, thir; but I wath to play on it thith year. I wath to be either tackle or quarterback. Latht year I wath a thubthithoot."

"Oh, indeed! That means a good deal, if the St. Maure's team is all that it is cracked up to be. I am surprised that you did not go back to St. Maure's to share in the glory of the team."

"I would go back, thir, only I want more

time and thecluthion for thtudieth."

Mr. Keenan was edified. As he had been at Milwaukee for only four weeks, it is not surprising that he had as yet learned nothing of Willie Hardy, who had not returned to St. Maure's because he had been "requested" by the vice president to stay at home.

"Well," said the prefect, "we might try you for our football eleven. The withdrawal of Archer leaves us short of a man, and perhaps we could play you in the line. The boys attending here of sufficient weight for the line of rushers are all of them either already engaged on the team, or for one reason or another cannot play."

"Couldn't I play quarterback?"

"We will see about that. Ah! There goes the bell for the football meeting. Come along with me, Willie." Mr. Keenan added, speaking rather to himself, "I expect to encounter a storm or two before we adjourn."

Chapter II

IN WHICH THE MILWAUKEE COLLEGE ELEVEN
BEGIN TO FEEL THE IRON HAND OF DISCIPLINE

NEARLY a score of boys were seated on the benches which lined the gymnasium. Facing them stood Mr. Keenan, in his hand a little notebook.

"Young gentlemen," he began, "I find that of last year's team, six are still attending college, namely, Harry Archer, quarterback; Claude Lightfoot, fullback; Walter Collins, left end; Andrew O'Neil, right end; John Drew, right guard; and Ernest Snowden, right halfback. I regret to say that Harry Archer does not intend to play football this year."

Something very like a groan came from the listeners.

"We might as well give up, then," said O'Neil ruefully.

"And then, again," laughed Mr. Keenan, "we mightn't. In the bright lexicon of football there's no such expression as 'give up.' Now, the new players suggested by a board of three college students, members of last year's team, are Charlie Pierson, of Poetry, as center rush; Gerald O'Rourke, of Poetry, as right tackle; Dan Dockery, of the same class, as left halfback; Frank Stein, of Poetry, as left guard; and Maurice Desmond, of Poetry, as left tackle. As you see, we now have no one for quarterback. Has anyone any suggestions to offer?"

"It seems to me, Mr. Keenan," said Gerald O'Rourke, "that Desmond might be trained for quarterback. He is very quick and rather light for the line. He is a good runner, and last year he played quarter for the second eleven."

"Second the motion!" said Pierson.

"It's the best we can do, I think," added another, while all the boys except Desmond and Willie Hardy nodded their heads in assent.

"Very good," Mr. Keenan said, as he made a note. "Now the next question is, whom shall we take for left tackle? Willie Hardy informs me that he was to have played on the celebrated St. Maure's team, had he returned. Certainly, he appears to be heavy enough."

Many of the boys looked at Willie doubtfully. There was a slight pause. Good-natured Claude came to the rescue.

"I think, sir," he said, that Willie might make a good tackle. When he was here before, he was one of our best runners, and he's pretty strong too."

"It wouldn't do any harm to give him a

trial," added O'Neil, "especially as we have so few to choose from. This year we have no good ball players to fall back on except three or four in the second team, who are all very light; and, as it is, our rush line will be under one hundred and forty-five pounds, and the lightest in the city."

"I weigh about one hundred and ninety-five poundth," put in Willie, with his ingenuous smile.

"I suppose you would weigh that if you were dressed in a couple of feather beds with dumbbell attachments," laughed Gerald O'Rourke. "At any rate, you are over one hundred and fifty, I believe, and if you're not afraid, doubtless you'll do very well."

Willie looked injured.

"A thudent from Thaint Maureth," he cried, glancing out of the corner of his eye at Mr. Keenan, who had attended that seat of learning in his youth, "fearth nothing!"

The listeners applauded this remark lustily; and half in joke, half in earnest, they agreed to allow Willie the position of left tackle.

"So now we have fixed our team conditionally. However, as we are not going to take up football in exactly the same way as last year, it will be well for each one of you to know what he is expected to do and what not to do. In the first place, there is to be practice regularly every afternoon, rain or shine; after class on Mondays, Tuesdays and Fridays, for half an hour; on Wednesdays and Saturdays for at least one hour; or, in place of that, a practice game. Again, every Thursday afternoon, which is your holiday, each one of you must report here at three o'clock for an hour or two of hard practice."

"I don't think I can come on Thursdays," said Snowden.

"Indeed! I am very sorry; but if you can't come, let me know tomorrow. We must have an eleven made up of players who practice together every day in the week, except Sunday. Last year, I am told, you didn't have your full team practicing together more than one time out of five. As a result, you were beaten badly on one occasion by the Centrals, a team which was, in material, by no means superior to your eleven. They had discipline and teamwork on their side, however."

"I guess I can manage to come," said Snowden, in a sulky voice.

"Is there anyone else who can't come?" continued Mr. Keenan.

The young man who had to attend to piano lessons twice a week, and that other who took private instruction in German and who, in consequence, had found it impossible to practice regularly with the team the preceding season, then and there concluded to do the impossible. The pianist, Rob Collins, however, resolved to speak.

"I have music lessons twice a week, just after class," he said.

"Indeed! Do you pay the teacher, or does he pay you?"

"I pay him."

"Well, I think he will be willing to change his hour for you, if you insist upon it. Of course, if he can't, we shall have to let you go."

"Oh, he'll change the time, if I put it in that way to him."

The boys were now looking at each other with eyes and mouths of astonishment. That Mr. Keenan should without a tremor give two of the oldest players the alternative of regular practice or leaving the football team was to their minds a bold proceeding. But there were further surprises in store for them.

"Another point! I understand, boys, that last year several members of the team were hard smokers."

"None of the fellowth on the team at Thaint

Maureth ever thmoked," interpolated Willie.

"I smoke," said Snowden sulkily, "and it doesn't hurt my playing."

"So do I," said Drew.

"And I," said Collins.

All of them spoke boldly.

"Is there any other smoker?" asked the prefect mildly.

"I 'hit' a pipe now and then," said Pierson. "But I am perfectly willing to stop, if you wish."

"I can't stop!" cried Collins.

"I won't," muttered Ernest Snowden. It was a whisper which reached the ear for which it was obviously intended.

"Well, young gentlemen, you have to do one of two things—stop smoking within a week, or leave the football team. Of course, nearly every boy who smokes will claim that it doesn't hurt him. Now, I am not prepared to say that every growing young man who smokes very moderately is injuring himself, but I am quite sure that the vast majority are the worse for their smoking. While I should regret to give up having a football eleven to represent our college, I should much prefer that course than to have an eleven without discipline. I regard football as the greatest of all games, principally for the reason that it schools a boy to almost heroic self-restraint both on and off the field. But when there is no discipline, there is no restraint—at least there is none off the field, and so one half of the good that should be obtained from the game is lost. And when there is no discipline, there is likely to be no teamwork on the field itself; and, again, instead of having headwork in the game, we have guesswork; and instead of team play, we have horseplay. Rather than allow such a state of things to go on, I will either abandon the idea of having a college eleven or I will fill up the vacancies with boys of the lower classes. This last course will ruin our prospect of victory for the present year, but in the following season, we should have a team worthy of the college. Now, what have the smokers to say?"

"I'll stop," said Walter Collins cheerfully.

Drew and Snowden were whispering together.

"Well, Drew?"

Drew was about to speak when Snowden touched him on the arm.

"If you please," said Snowden, "Drew and I would like to think about it before we give any answer."

There was a touch of rebellion in the boy's manner.

"Well, in this case," said Mr. Keenan, "the boy who hesitates is lost. If you don't care about putting that much restraint on yourselves, you are either inveterate smokers, and then we don't want you; or you are too indifferent to the good of the eleven to make a sacrifice. In either case, I don't want you."

"I'll stop," said Drew.

"And I won't," muttered Snowden.

"Then, Mr. Snowden, you are excused from further attendance at this meeting."

Snowden put his hands in his pockets and walked out.

The boys looked very gloomy. Snowden had been one of the best players on the preceding year's team.

"I am very sorry, boys," said Mr. Keenan, "to have begun the season with so much unpleasantness, but I made up my mind before coming here to have a disciplined team or none at all. Some of you may think that I am too exacting; but you will learn in the long run, I think, that I am looking to your good and the good name and honor of the college.

"I am told that last year even the old boys, that is, our former students, were disgusted with the loose playing of the college eleven. While your opponents during the halves of the game gathered together comparing notes

and planning for the last half, five or six of
your players were hidden in various corners
or behind fences, smoking the deadly cigarette or pulling at a pipe. The players you
went against did none of these things for
the simple reason that their paid coach
wouldn't hear of such irregularities. They
were paying him a hundred dollars or so
monthly to forbid them just such things.
Now, you boys have no paid coach; but I'm
going to do for nothing what a coach would
do for a good salary."

"That's right," said Dockery. "Even the
small boys noticed how much more other
teams sacrificed than our boys for the sake
of the game."

"Don't you think, Mr. Keenan," inquired
Pierson, "that we could get one or two of the
old players to help us out?"

"No," said Mr. Keenan emphatically. "I don't
want a single player who is not a *bona fide*
student of Milwaukee College. My first reason is that, as a rule, such a player cannot
attend regular practice; again, we cannot be
quite so sure that he keeps in regular training; in the third place, he is not under the
discipline of the college and he may play a
style of game which the authorities do not
approve of. Finally, he is not a college stu-

dent, and football, as it is now played, is a game for college students. Hence, we shall play no game with athletic associations, no game with outside teams which are not under the direct sanction and control of some responsible school or college. Football is essentially a young gentlemen's game. It is quite feasible, at times, to play a game of baseball with rough characters; but in football, you must play only with gentlemen—otherwise the game becomes a slugging match and a question as to which is the better or worse set of rowdies.] Now the next point is the election of captain. We need no formalities. Dan Dockery will pass around the slips of paper which I have provided him with, and each one of you will write the name of him whom you wish to be captain."

"According to the votes," announced Dockery a few minutes later, "Claude Lightfoot has eight, Dan Dockery one, and Ernest Snowden one."

"Therefore," added Mr. Keenan, "Claude Lightfoot is Captain."

Mr. Keenan was guilty of a rash judgment on this occasion. He concluded that Drew had cast his vote for Snowden, but the voter in question was none other than Willie Hardy.

"Is there any further business, boys?"

Claude arose.

"I want to thank the fellows, Mr. Keenan, for electing me. I don't think I am particularly fitted to be captain, but I'll do my best; and I think, too, that even if our team is weaker individually than last year's, we will play a much better game, provided we follow your instructions."

The boys applauded Claude, as, covered with blushes, he seated himself.

"Mr. Keenan," said Dockery, "what about our diet?"

The prefect smiled.

"I had intended," he said, "to lay down a few rules; but you boys have taken my remarks about smoking and regular practice so hard that I am afraid to say anything more."

"We're all converted," said Walter Collins. "Please give us a few instructions."

"Yes."—"That's right."—"Go on, sir."

In some inexplicable way, the boys had changed from shadow to sunshine. Mr. Keenan, who in the first ten minutes of the meeting had aroused little but opposition, had, since the withdrawal of Snowden, secured their full confidence.

"Well, I'll give you a very simple regulation. Eat three hearty meals a day, eat nothing between meals, avoid ice cream and cakes.

For the rest, stay at home of nights, and go to bed before ten."

Everyone looked pleased.

"Shall we promise to do it, boys?" inquired Claude.

"I promith!" cried Willie Hardy.

Then each and every boy followed Willie's example, and each and every one with the exception of Willie meant what he said.

Meeting adjourned.

Chapter III

IN WHICH IT IS SHOWN THAT THE GAME OF FOOTBALL, WITH ITS SEVERE PREPARATORY WORK, HAS MANY POINTS IN ITS FAVOR

MILWAUKEE College, like all Gaul, is divided into three parts: the college building itself, on Tenth, and facing State Street; the playground proper, very large, very bare, destitute of grass; and, separated from the College by a strip of land and a plank walk, "the college green," the third part, a sacred place which no student may set foot upon without express permission. It is the one ambition of John, the faithful college janitor, to keep this "green" true to its name; and it is the ever-present disappointment of his life that he meets with but partial success; for in the football season, the eleven use it for their practice ground, and in spring the fielders of the baseball nine invade it, while the small boy who hopes in later years to be himself a player stands without the boundary mark and looks wistful—or, mayhap, should the prefect disappear—desecrates the reserve with his unhallowed foot.

After the football meeting, the ten players, throwing aside their coats, entered the "green" and were about to tackle and run in the usual violent fashion when Mr. Keenan interposed.

"Hold on, boys," he said: "this won't do at all. Some of you are utterly out of training; probably not more than two of your number are in any kind of condition for such work as hard tackling and running. You must begin gently, or someone may be hurt. Even supposing none of you were hurt, there would be several of you too stiff and sore to practice tomorrow. Suppose you form a ring, standing three yards apart from each other."

Mr. Keenan was pleased with their alacrity

in falling into the position suggested. It was evident to him that he had gained the boys' confidence.

"Now, Lightfoot, begin by passing the ball to your neighbor, and throw it slowly."

Lightfoot, holding the ball in his hand with the long axis resting upon his forearm, passed it to the player at his right by swinging the full length of his arm, inclined a little from the level of the shoulder. Pierson caught the oval and passed it with both hands to his neighbor, who in turn passed it until, finally, the ball was returned to Claude.

"It won't do," said Mr. Keenan.

"I thought tho," Willie remarked to Gerald O'Rourke.

"What's wrong, sir?" asked Claude.

"In passing the ball, Claude, where do you want the runner to receive it?"

"Anywhere he can catch it, I suppose."

"But is there a best place?"

"Why, now that I come to think of it, I should suppose that the one who passes the ball ought to aim at the waist of the fellow who is to catch it."

"Exactly. Suppose a halfback is running up against the line; he should be advancing head down. If you aim at his waist, he gets the ball exactly where it is easiest to catch it without losing speed or changing position. Now, try again, and use both hands and one arm in passing, as that is the best and quickest way for short passes."

"That's a new point for me," said O'Neil in a whisper to O'Rourke.

"For me, too; Mr. Keenan must have been a football player in his day."

This time, although the boys were more careful in passing the ball, several of them were slow and awkward.

"Now throw the ball harder," said Mr. Keenan, as presently in the course of their practice they showed more ease in their movements. "Anyone who misses must fall on the ball."

Willie Hardy and Charlie Pierson were obliged to fall on the ball in this round, to the great amusement of the small boys standing outside the forbidden ground and gazing on the scene with open mouths and rounded eyes. Looking at the players, one would think that their holding the ball was a matter of life or death. Andrew O'Neil, at the beginning of the practice, had remarked that he did not believe in "baby work." He was now perspiring, partly from the exercise, partly from fear of a false throw or a muff. Even the little things of football are to be done carefully.

When about seven or eight minutes had been spent in this exercise, Mr. Keenan called a halt.

"Where are you going, Pierson?" he asked, as the future center rush made at a trot toward the college building.

"To get a drink, sir."

"I think you can afford to wait: no drinking during practice."

"What does he take us for?" inquired Stein of Maurice Desmond.

"For a lot of geese," answered Maurice, with a grin. "And he's about right."

"Yes," assented Collins. "And I'm glad he's coming down on us. Last year we all felt that more discipline was needed, and yet we wouldn't submit to it unless it was forced upon us. It's about time for us to go to work and saw wood."

As Pierson returned somewhat shame-faced, Mr. Keenan whispered to him:

"That is all right, Charlie—offer it up."

Charlie, who was the best-natured boy in the college, broke into a smile. His good humor was at once restored.

"Now, boys, we must begin to get ready for running. There's no need of practicing on the green for this particular exercise. Range yourselves in single file beside the parallel bars and trot slowly along the fence all the way around. Claude, you take the lead and be careful not to go fast."

They had no sooner started than, with refreshing alacrity, every small boy in the yard fell into line, with the result that the file of runners was fully fifty yards in length, and, owing to the hilarious cries and motions of the knickerbockered tribe, formed a very inspiring scene to the prefect and the various knots of spectators without and within the college enclosure.

While Mr. Keenan, thus rapt in pleasant contemplation, was standing beside the parallel bars, Snowden, who had been a gloomy witness thus far of the first practice, advanced and touched his cap.

"Mr. Keenan," he said, "I'd like to apologize. I was out of humor this afternoon and made a fool of myself. If you'll overlook what has happened, I'll promise not to smoke anymore."

The runners were nearing the two. Pierson, who was fat, was blowing heavily, and pretty Willie Hardy had lost his smile.

"Halt!" cried the prefect. "Well, Snowden, you may fall into line. Once more, Claude,

but even a little slower, and stop halfway—
that is, when you come opposite home base.
I notice that a couple of your men are almost
winded. When you reach the base, walk back
here."

His directions were followed to the letter.

"Tomorrow, boys," announced Mr. Keenan
on their return, "I shall put you directly
under charge of your captain, Claude Lightfoot. He and I shall have a talk together
now and arrange upon what is best to be
done. Those who wish to play on our eleven
must obey him in what regards football on
and off the field."

Claude and the prefect held a long conference, and the boy with whom athletics
were almost a second nature seemed to catch
by intuition the general plan of campaign
which Mr. Keenan was outlining.

"I think, sir," he said, "that we can make
it go. There will be no trouble with the new
players, and none with Collins and O'Neill.
They are all willing to learn. The only fellows who may growl are Ernest Snowden
and Drew. Both of them belonged to a crowd
in last year's team who thought that all they
had to do in football was to go in and win.
They were great big fellows, and because they
could block their opponents easily and do a

few things which depend more on strength and weight than anything else, they thought that they were fine football players."

"Whereas," supplemented Mr. Keenan, "they were merely fine material."

"Yes; they were that sure," assented Claude.

"That's a point which shows how young football really is in the West, Claude; it is quite possible for a boy to play three or four years in a college team, and think himself a fine player, without his really knowing the rudiments of the game."

"I'm beginning to think, sir, after what you've said, that none of us here knows the rudiments. If I try to follow your directions, the boys will have to practice a great deal of real self-denial."

"It will do them good."

"Mr. Keenan," said Claude with a laugh, "I've often been amused by the way boys make sacrifices for the sake of a field day or a football game. Now, last year the boys of the Central High School eleven who beat us so badly dieted severely, went to bed early, gave up smoking, ate and drank nothing between meals, got up early and gave up lots of delicacies in the eating and drinking line. The day before they played us, several of them were going to a party, and when their captain sent them word that they could not go, they gave it up. They were awfully afraid of our team, and our team wasn't a bit afraid of them. You've heard, of course, how they beat us twenty-six to nothing. Well, here's the thing that amused me. Those fellows, for the sake of winning a game, practiced mortification and self-denial enough almost to make them saints. If they had done all that for the love of God it would raise them, I reckon, to a high degree of holiness."

Mr. Keenan laughed.

"Well, Claude, I am glad you spoke of that. Didn't it ever occur to you that you could combine the two things? All the sacrifices you make for the sake of a football game may count in the supernatural order too."

Claude opened his eyes to their widest.

"I don't quite see," he remarked.

"Don't you belong to the League of the Sacred Heart?"

"Yes, sir; I think every boy in the college is a member. This year I have been appointed a Promoter and have charge of a band of fifteen, all in the Poetry class. All the football players of my class are in my band."

"Splendid!" cried Mr. Keenan with enthusiasm. "Now, Claude, as you are a Promoter, and have half, or more than half, of the football team under your care, you can do ever so much to make the League devotion practical."

"I'd be very glad to do anything I could, sir. But I don't understand yet."

"Well, you know the Morning Offering, don't you?"

"Yes, sir. Every morning we offer all our thoughts, words and actions of the day in union with the interests of the Sacred Heart."

"Just so; now how many kinds of actions are there?"

"Three, sir: good actions, bad actions and indifferent actions."

"What is a good action?"

"An action, sir, that by its very nature pleases God; as, for instance, to pray, to do a kind act for the love of God, to resist a temptation."

"And what is a bad action?"

"An action, sir, which by its very nature is offensive to God, as to steal, to blaspheme, to lie."

"Now what is an indifferent action?"

"An action which in itself is neither bad nor good; as to eat dinner, to walk, to run, to read, or to stand on your head."

"I congratulate you on your knowledge of

the catechism, Claude. What kind of action is football?"

"It is a bully action, sir!" said Claude, with a laugh. "But looking at it from the way we study our catechism, I should say that it is neither bad nor good in itself and, consequently, indifferent."

"So, then, football playing is neither bad nor good."

"I guess not, sir; it's good!" said Claude fervently.

"Then it's not indifferent."

"No, sir."

"Aren't you getting confused, Claude?"

"Well," returned the captain of the eleven, "it's this way. If a boy plays football for a good end, it's a good action. If he plays for a bad end, it's a bad action."

"But," argued Mr. Keenan, "football is a bad action, and I'll prove it. A game where there is slugging and ill temper and revenge is made up of bad actions. But in football we have slugging and ill temper and revenge. Therefore football is made up of bad actions."

Claude was not a philosopher, so he failed to answer this objection "in form."

"What you say does not seem to be true, Mr. Keenan. Slugging is positively forbidden in football, and revenge has nothing to do

with any game. As regards ill temper, it is
the same in football as in any other game:
the boy who loses his temper plays all the
worse, as a rule. So, you see, those things
you speak of are an abuse and don't belong
to the game at all."

"Right again, Claude: football, so far from
being a game for the promotion of rowdi-
ness, is a game where a player is schooled
to control his passions under the utmost
provocation. It is hard to say whether, if
rightly played, football does more for one's
bravery than for one's endurance. The people who cry out against football as being a
game for the promotion of savagery are simply confounding the game itself with some
abuses which threaten to creep in. We are
both satisfied, then, that the game is indifferent. Now the next question is, how can it
be made bad?"

"I suppose, sir, it would be made bad for
an individual player if he were to play for
some bad end: for instance to show off, or
to revenge himself on someone else."

"And how could it be made good?"

"Easily, sir. If a boy were to exclude all
bad motives and were to offer it up with his
other actions of the day, it would become a
good act."

"Hence it is quite possible for a boy to play a hard football game, to enjoy himself immensely and, at the same time, to please and honor the Sacred Heart very much."

"Good gracious!" said Claude. "Then I've been having a lot of fun in football and at the same time have been doing good for my soul. It seems so funny, sir; I can't imagine it."

"I thought you would say something like that, Claude. It does look strange on the face of it. But I think that I can make the matter clearer for you. Suppose a man were to come to our water faucet outside and take a drink of water. There would be no harm and no good in the action of drinking—would there?"

"No, sir."

"But suppose that before drinking, he should propose to signify by that action his hatred of God, wouldn't that intention make it a bad act?"

"Of course it would. I think, sir, that he would sin mortally."

"So do I. Now God is more willing to be pleased than to be displeased, quicker to reward than punish. Hence, if he were to offer up the action of drinking the water to show his love for God, it would follow that his action would be a good one, and one for which he would get a reward."

"That's a consoling doctrine, sir."

"Indeed it is, and a very practical one too. So if you boys submit to hard training and discipline, you can offer every one of those acts each day to the Sacred Heart, and the harder the discipline and training come on your natural inclinations, the more merit will you gain, the better boys will you become."

"That's fine!" cried Claude, jumping to his feet. "Just think! Every bump I get can be offered up for my sins. I'm going to talk this over with the Poetry boys on my team, and I'll get Harry Collins to attend to it with the other fellows, and I'm sure they'll all be delighted to join football training and devotion to the Sacred Heart together."

"I believe so, too, Claude, and the better you practice devotion to the Sacred Heart, the better you will play football. Halloa! It is nearly five o'clock. Go home to your studies, young man, and when you're working at them, remember that they too can be rendered very meritorious by the Morning Offering."

And Claude literally skipped home. Doubtless he skipped with a good intention too.

Chapter IV

THE HOME OF HARRY ARCHER

WHILE the boys in single file, and to the admiration of all beholders, were trotting leisurely around the college ground, Harry Archer was making his way westward on Fond du Lac Avenue to his home. It was a walk of over two miles; but Harry, on this occasion at least, took no note of its length, for he was busy with his thoughts.

It was a bitter, bitter thing to give up playing on the football team, and now that the sacrifice had been made, he would have felt utterly miserable were it not for the hope that Mr. Keenan had held out to him of having a great mathematician to assist him in preparing for the *Evening Wisconsin* Mathematical Contest. When Harry first read the announcement concerning this contest, in the preceding month of August, he had at once resolved to take part in it. On the same day, he took out of the bookcase Wentworth's *Geometry* and set to work at reviewing the books which he had already seen in class.

Within a week, a strange thing, as Harry regarded it, came to pass. He discovered that a strong liking for mathematics had supplanted his former passive indifference. During his year in the class of Humanities, he had studied moderately, had taken but little interest in the problems, and yet at the end of the season had passed a creditable examination, but far inferior to Claude Lightfoot's and a little below the work of O'Rourke and Desmond. But now he loved the study; and the preparation for the contest which he had entered into without much thought of winning or losing had quickly ceased to be a task and developed into an enthusiasm. He began to feel his power; and with the prospect of an expert's help, the future, despite his abandonment of football, became bright. Oh, if he could but gain the prize! Aside from the honor to himself and to his college, there were the eighty dollars! It was the money chiefly that Harry was looking for. And yet, as we shall presently see, he was anything but of a mercenary disposition.

Harry entered his home, then, by no means despondent. He tripped lightly up the stairs into the living room, where he stopped suddenly, while his face took on an expression of dismay.

A woman clothed in black was seated at a table on which were paper and other writing materials. Her face was bent down upon the table, her hands were clasped over her head, and her whole form was quivering. There was no need of surmise to know that she was in a passion of grief, for her sobs left no doubt.

"Why, Mother!" exclaimed Harry.

Mrs. Archer raised her face, wet with tears, and looked quite alarmed. She had been taken by surprise.

Before she could say a word, Harry bent over and kissed her with unusual tenderness in his manner and unusual sympathy upon his honest face.

"Have you been thinking of Father?" he inquired.

"Yes, Harry, but I am resigned to his loss. I have also been thinking of you and your sister Alice and little Paul, and I am afraid I lost courage for the moment. But I didn't want you to know anything about it, my dear."

"Something has happened, then. You must tell me, Mother. After all," Harry added with a smile, "I'm the man of the family. Has anything gone wrong today?"

"Yes, Harry. I thought we had fairly cleared off all our debts, when a new bill came in today. It's for eight-five dollars, and had to be paid."

"And didn't you have the money?"

"Yes; I had been saving up to pay the one hundred and five dollars' interest on our mortgage which falls due in early December, and I had already laid by ninety dollars; now there are but five dollars left, and I see no way of getting the money together between this time and December. And so, Harry, I fear we shall be compelled to lose our home."

"Isn't there any way out at all, Mother?"

"No, dear, unless we sell the piano. But I can hardly bring myself to think of taking it from Alice. It's the one possession of hers in the house which she really loves. Besides, she needs it to keep up her practice and for giving her music lessons."

"There's no question about it," said Harry, with the air of a man. "The piano shall not be sold. I'll go to work first. Don't you think, Mother, that I ought to give up school at once?"

"If it were not for our hopes in the silver mine stock, Harry, I should be forced to take you away. Indeed, my boy, were it not for the chance that our shares would be of some value, I do not see how in conscience I could have allowed you to return to college at all. But since the opening of school, the most discouraging reports have reached me. At present, our shares are not worth much more than the paper used for them, and the hope of their rising in value is growing fainter and fainter. And now this sudden call on me for so large a sum of money makes me wonder whether I can keep you at college. You know, my dear, how eager your father was for you to complete the classical course, and how I share that eagerness. I cannot bring myself to think of your leaving college, and yet I'm afraid, Harry, that unless God comes to our help, we shall have to take you away. In the meantime, though, keep on. There is no reason for leaving before you have made sure of a position. Besides, your schooling until January has been paid for in advance, and who knows but that in some way or other things may grow brighter. I may get more copying to do, and Alice may find a few more pupils. Let us keep on praying."

"That's right, Mother. And please don't cry anymore. By the way, after this I am going to earn a dollar and a half a week."

Mrs. Archer looked at her boy in surprise.

"I'm going to carry the *Evening Wisconsin,* Mother. And I have a fine route. It is practically on my way home and won't interfere with my college work at all. You see, right after school, beginning tomorrow, I shall run down to the office, get my pack of papers and deliver them on my way here, so that I'll be back by half-past four, or, at the very latest, five. It will give me just enough exercise to keep me going."

"But Harry, what about your football?"

"I'm not going to play this year, Mother."

Harry said this with an attempt at indifference; but his mother, who knew how her boy loved the game, who had heard him talk about it and seen him even study it, understood what a sacrifice he had made. There was a tear in her eye again, but it was a tear of gratitude. Poverty for the moment lost its blackness, care its heaviness, the future its gloom in the presence of her son's sacrifice of love. Upon my word, if boys knew what their affection and duty to their parents could bring about, there would be a wondrous change for the better in this world. The generations would become longer-lived, the face of many a mother, now drawn with grief and aged with care, would grow bright and cheerful, while the heart within would be strong to bear the bitterest trials in the strength of the son's dutiful love.

"Harry," said the mother, rising and laying her hand as though in benediction upon her boy's head, "I should never have asked you to make the sacrifice. May God reward you, my darling boy."

And Harry, who, like most boys of seventeen, hated anything like the display of the more tender emotions, simply bowed his head and hurried from the room.

Under the stairway on the first floor was a small apartment for odds and ends. Harry opened the door and brought out into the hallway his bicycle, bought for him by his father just three months ago.

He gazed at it mournfully.

"So I shall have to let you go, too. It's too bad," he soliloquized.

And again he gazed upon his beloved bicycle mournfully. Poor Harry, having sacrificed his football, had counted upon taking his pleasure and exercise upon the wheel. Naturally good at athletics, he had hoped to take a high place among the bicyclists of Milwaukee College at the field day in the ensuing spring. But now the bright visions which he had conjured up were rudely but voluntarily dispelled. It was a question of sacrificing Alice's piano or his wheel. It is true, the piano would bring in a larger sum and enable Mrs. Archer to pay the interest on the mortgage without difficulty, but Harry was resolved that the piano should be kept, so long as there was the slightest hope of meeting their obligations otherwise.

"Well," he reflected, "I suppose I can stand it, for the sake of Alice and my mother. But I am awfully sorry for Paul. He expects me to teach him this week."

"Are you going out for a ride, Harry?" cried Paul, a chubby boy of eight, as he came tripping into the hallway with a large bundle done up in brown paper under his arm.

"No, Paul, but I was thinking of teaching you how to ride."

Paul made a plunge into the air, then darted toward the kitchen with a whoop of joy.

He came back at a gallop, and the two with the bicycle between them repaired to the yard.

For half an hour, Harry continued to teach his brother. The wheel was somewhat too large for the little fellow, but notwithstanding this disadvantage, he succeeded eventually in going five or six yards unaided.

"First rate, Paul. In one more lesson you will be a graduate. All you will need after that will be a little practice."

"And you'll let me practice on your wheel, won't you, Harry, whenever you're not using it yourself?"

"I'm afraid not, Paul. I think I shall sell my wheel."

Paul gazed at his brother with great eyes.

"Well, then you'll buy me a wheel for myself, won't you, Harry? You told me you would try to do everything for me that Papa would do, if he were alive; and I know Papa would buy me a wheel."

"Yes, but Papa knew how to make money for you, Paul, and I don't. But just wait for a little while, and I'll get you a nice wheel, too, as soon as I can afford it."

"Will it be long, Harry?"

"I hope not, but it will be good to wait for a while. If you were to get one now, you would grow so fast in a year that you would need another one very soon. I think we had better wait till you grow a little."

"Yes," assented Paul brightly, "and I'll save up in my bank and help you pay. I say, Harry, we ought to change our grocer."

"Why?"

"He doesn't give me cakes or candy any more when I go to buy things there for Mama. And then he used to smile and make me laugh, and now he looks as cross as you do when you play football."

Harry smiled at the comparison, but he felt once more the sting of poverty. The grocer had altered since the death of his father. Soon it would be the same with the butcher and the baker. Harry looked upon these changes as misfortunes. He was mistaken. As far as he was concerned, the change from comparative wealth to comparative poverty was a blessing.

Chapter V

SHOWING HOW A WANT OF READY MONEY IS NOT ALWAYS A THING TO BE DEPLORED

HARRY, it was said in the last chapter, was mistaken in looking upon the change from comparative wealth to comparative poverty as a misfortune. To make this statement intelligible to the reader, it is necessary to go back to a somewhat earlier period of his life.

Four months before, that is, in May of the preceding school year, Harry Archer was a student of Humanities and the captain and catcher of the college baseball club. As a captain he was quite good; as a catcher he was considered one of the best among the amateurs of the city; as a student of Humanities he was slightly below the average. And yet it was patent to all that Harry was a boy of more than ordinary intellectual ability. His teacher knew this from the intelligent questions which Harry often put to him; his prefects knew it from the quickness and head-work which he displayed in all athletic contests; his companions knew it from the skill with which he directed them in plays where brain counted for more than brawn.

How was it then that Harry held so poor a place in the classroom? There were various answers. Certain members of the college faculty attributed his poor record to a want of imagination. There was no originality in his work. But they failed to distinguish between a want of imagination and a dormant imagination. Harry's reading was confined almost entirely to the athletic columns of the daily paper. He knew the records of all the great bicycle riders, the weight, height, and abilities of most of the leading football players in the great eastern colleges and in the local elevens; he was perfectly acquainted with the relative standing of the professional baseball teams in four different leagues. In a word, his readings, though, viewed from

the standpoint of morality, of the most innocent order, were such as did nothing to develop
his literary gifts, while at the same time they
enriched—or rather pauperized—him with a
vocabulary which goes very well in an ordinary newspaper, but which is, by its very
nature, positively harmful to the development
of a fine imagination and a good style.
Whether or not, therefore, Harry was lack-
ing in fancy was a question which could not
be answered. A beautiful imagination may
be a sleeping beauty.

Other members of the college faculty,
accordingly, who knew the scope and substance of Harry's reading, accounted for his
poor class standing in a different way. His
teacher in the class of Humanities attributed it to his love of athletic sports. "When
a boy gives all his energies to athletics," he
had once said, "you can hardly expect him
to have anything left for studies."

The teacher, in making this statement,
was perfectly correct. But his suppressed
minor was wrong. He implied that Harry
gave all his energy to athletics. As a matter of fact, Harry returned to his home every
afternoon in the year quite fresh and full of
animal spirits. After supper—a very hearty
one invariably—he went out four or five

times in the week to visit his friends. When he did not go out himself, he stayed at home to "receive."

They were lively boys, these friends of Harry's, neither particularly bad nor particularly good. Most of them, as it happened, were non-Catholics, and most of them, as was the case with Harry, had as yet no object in life. Now anyone who is at all acquainted with the methods of teaching which obtain in our Catholic colleges must know that the boy who plays after school and goes out visiting his friends at nightfall cannot possibly do justice to his studies. He might as well try to burn a candle at three ends. Hence those who, with the teacher, attributed Harry's ill success to athletics ignored an important factor of that ill success.

Harry's prefect of the preceding year had hit upon what I consider the true solution. On one occasion he said to the boy:

"I would advise you to stay at home every night. Give at least one hour and a half to your studies, an hour to the reading of good books, and then you will hold a place in the class very near if not equal to Claude Lightfoot's."

Harry on the spot resolved to turn over a new leaf. But, I am sorry to say, he was too weak to adhere to his resolution. His mother, it is true, endeavored to persuade him to remain at home, but he was under a divided allegiance. Mr. Archer was a doting father. He loved his boy foolishly. Rather than cause Harry the least disappointment, he would allow him anything that was not forbidden by the moral law. Moreover, as Mr. Archer was making a comfortable living, it was in his power to gratify Harry even to the point of extravagance. He would not allow his children to do any work about the house. They were to run no messages, to do no chores, to have no responsibility of any kind. In a word, Harry's training, so far as his father was concerned in it, should have made the boy utterly selfish, effeminate and self-willed. These effects, however, were partially counteracted by the mother's influence, partially by athletics.

It was upon the diamond and upon the gridiron that Harry was taught the bitter-sweet lesson of self-control, of yielding to the judgment of others, of effacing for the time being his own personality and of identifying himself with the interests of all; of restraining his temper when the game went against him, and, not unfrequently, of facing pains and hurts with cheerful courage. If Harry did possess some traits of manliness, it was in spite of his father.

But after everything has been said, the fact remains that he was very selfish; that he looked upon every day of his life as consisting of twenty-four hours which were, each of them, to be killed; that lessons were enemies to be avoided; that the present day, and the present day only, was to be considered. There was but little promise, four months ago, in the future that lay before him. He needed an awakening; and the awakening came.

In the beginning of June his father died, after an illness of nine days. Mr. Archer had lived up to his income, and, though a fair businessman, had been strangely improvident. One week before his final sickness, to give an instance, his insurance policy for ten thousand dollars had run out, and he had neglected to renew it.

After his death, it was discovered that his affairs were in a very involved condition; and when the lawyers had done their work and pocketed their fees, Mrs. Archer found herself facing the world with a few dollars and a home straddled by a heavy mortgage.

Harry loved his mother tenderly. On learning of their altered condition, a change came over him at once. He felt that it was his duty to take charge of the family. He forgot himself. The friends whom formerly he could not be persuaded to abandon, he now gave up of his own accord. To go with them meant to spend money, and Harry now had no money.

During the preceding vacation he worked as clerk in a wholesale hardware house at a salary of six dollars a week. His sister Alice, who had just graduated at the Academy of the Holy Angels, succeeded in securing two pupils on the piano. Mrs. Archer, having dismissed the two servants, took charge of the house herself and, at odd times, did some copying for a lawyer who was an old friend of the family.

On returning to college in September, Harry was resolved to make the most of what would probably be his last session at school. He looked back with regret upon the years which he had wasted and was determined to make up for lost time as far as was in his power. And from the very first day of class, it became evident to him that the coming year was to be a year of sacrifice. If he wished to study faithfully and to help his mother, he must abandon athletics. Besides, to take part in athletics involved the paying out now and then of small sums of money.

So Harry, after a cruel struggle, made his resolution. To clinch that resolution, to burn, as it were, his bridges after him, he secured a carrier's route on the *Evening Wisconsin*; and finally, as we saw in the last chapter, he resolved to make the last sacrifice—the sacrifice of his bicycle.

There was a boy in the neighborhood who for five months had been saving with the intention of buying a good wheel. Harry went to him and without the least difficulty secured forty dollars in cash for the bicycle, which but a few months before had been bought for seventy-five dollars.

Then Harry brought the money to his mother. Before Mrs. Archer could speak, he left the room. While the mother's eyes filled with tears of tenderness, Harry in his own room threw himself upon his bed utterly miserable.

He had made his sacrifice with the buoyant and noble enthusiasm of youth. But now the revulsion of feeling had come, and for the time being he was very unhappy. Doubtless this feeling of bitterness and misery was a blessing to the boy. Sacrifice ennobles and purifies the soul just in so far as it goes against our irrational feelings and vicious inclinations.

"Is that you, Harry?" cried Alice, looking into the room.

Harry sprang up and, with averted head, bade his sister come in.

"What is the matter, Harry? You needn't turn your face away; I can see that you are put out about something."

"I'm put out about almost everything," answered Harry, turning toward Alice with a smile which came with difficulty and looked rather disconcerted after it arrived, as though it felt out of place.

"Well, here's one thing you can't be put out about," said Alice, taking her brother's hand and smoothing it. "I received a new pupil today, and that makes three; and she's a nice little girl, and if I can succeed in getting three more, I shall be making a dollar and a half a day; and I am quite sure that I shall get three more. There, Harry, are you put out about that?"

"Alice, you're worth a dozen like me. Your good humor and courage alone are far more than a dollar a day to all of us. If it had not been for you, I think that we should all have fallen into despair long ago. Take the present moment; just before you entered I was thinking of nothing but the dark side of things, and just as soon as you began telling me your good news, I almost forgot everything unpleasant and suddenly remembered what was cheerful. First of all, I'm going to earn one dollar and a half every week for carrying the *Evening Wisconsin.* This isn't much, but at least it will keep me in clothes. Secondly—"

Alice interrupted him with a laugh.

"What are you laughing at now?" cried Harry, forcing a frown.

"Keep you in clothes!" cried Alice. "In shoes and stockings, you mean. Young athletes like that brother of mine can't play football and—"

"Hold on! But I'm not going to play football."

Alice sat down upon the bed.

"Well I never!" she exclaimed, raising her hands. "Harry, I'll never go to a game again."

"Oh, yes, you will. You will go with me to the game on Thanksgiving Day, and I'll show you how to root for our college in the proper way. You girls sit around and smile when we win or look distressed when we lose. That's not the way."

"I suppose, young gentleman, you want us convent girls to get up and yell your barbarous college yells. You want us to shout out 'Hiki, hiki, hai, kai—Muki mori, hai yai!' "

"No, I don't; and none of the college fellows expect you to do that sort of thing. We want the boys to attend to that part of the program themselves. Of course, we may be wrong about it, but we expect a certain amount of maidenly reserve from young ladies, even in the excitement of a football game, and—"

"Exactly," broke in Alice, secretly pleased with her brother's views. "All you mean to say is that you want to show me the way I ought to—to—"

"Root, Alice."

"Thank you, to root, in case I were a boy; and I do most solemnly wish I were a boy. Then I'd be head of this family and would support it, and I'd buy little Paul a bicycle."

"I've just sold mine and given the money to Mother."

Alice, who had arisen, sat down again.

"Laws!" she exclaimed. "No, I don't wish I was a boy"—and she caught Harry's hand and squeezed it with a grip which should have made him wince—"if I were, I wouldn't at all compare with you, you dear old fellow."

"Don't get sentimental, Alice," said Harry, returning the squeeze, whereat Alice gave a shriek, which showed that she had a very powerful alto voice, and aimed a playful blow at her brother's ear, which the sturdy young fellow dodged very easily.

Then both broke into a hearty laugh, in the ring of which there was neither hint nor shadow of trouble or of care.

While they were still laughing, Mrs. Archer entered the room.

"I like that kind of music," she said with a smile. "Has Harry told you all the wonderful things he has done today, Alice?"

"He is a hero today," said Alice, "and would be worth putting into a book if it weren't for his freckles and his sandy hair. Mother, I've a new pupil, and I'm just as happy as can be."

"The prettiest thing in nature," observed Harry, "is a sunbeam."

"That settles it, if you say so," cried Alice banteringly.

"Why, Harry?" asked the mother.

"I found it out just now. I was feeling blue just a minute ago when Alice came in and jollied me—"

"I beg your pardon," cried Alice, putting her hand to her ear.

"I mean, jollied me up—"

"Won't you translate?" persisted Alice.

"Oh, pshaw! Alice came in and began telling the good news and grinning—"

"Grinning, indeed!" muttered Alice.

"And now I feel as though a sunbeam had shot through my brain, and am as jolly as can be. Alice is a sunbeam and—"

"I thank you, kind sir," cried Miss Alice, with the sort of a bow which only convent graduates dare venture upon.

At this point of the conversation Paul came in, contentedly eating bread and butter. Seeing everyone smiling, he broke into a laugh.

"There's the best sunbeam in Milwaukee!" cried Alice, as she kissed the little man out of hand.

Chapter VI

IN WHICH MATHEMATICIANS ARE GIVEN THEIR DUE

"HEY there, Harry! Hold on for a moment!" bawled Claude Lightfoot on the corner of Thirteenth and State Streets at Harry Archer, who was within a few yards of Twelfth. Claude, as he was speaking, broke into a run and was upon Harry in a trice.

"I see you're in condition already," said

Harry, with a smile.

"I'm always in condition for a run," laughed Claude. "I say, Harry, you're not going to give up football?"

"I've got to. You needn't look so bad about it. I feel it worse than you can. Besides, you have plenty of good material."

"Not among the College boys, and no outsiders are allowed to join; and what's more, even if we had a choice of material, we have no one who can take your place as quarterback. You remember that trick play we were practicing last year, where you were to get the ball and go down the field with no one else around?"

"You mean the one we didn't have the chance to play, the one where you pass the ball on a long pass for over ten yards? It is a pity we had no chance to use it."

"I think," said Claude, "that if you were in the game, we would make a touchdown on it sure. But we can't do it without you. Then, again, we'll have to let all the plays go where the quarterback throws the ball to the runner—at least the long-distance plays. Even if we succeed in training Maurice Desmond to throw the ball accurately, we can't count on his doing it in his first games. He's a young player, and very nervous. Harry, you'll have to play quarterback."

"That's what I say!" cried Gerald O'Rourke, catching Claude's last remark as he came up with his two friends and classmates. "We can't do anything without you and with Willie Hardy. I passed him on Eleventh Street just now. He was in the candy store puffing at a cigarette. Come on, Harry, and join us, and then we'll drop Hardy like a hotcake."

"It's impossible, Gerald. You know I'd do anything for you or Claude—"

"That's right," put in Claude cheerily.

"But I can't play this year, and I wish you would ask the other fellows not to bother me about it. Here comes Hardy now."

"Helloa, fellowth!" cried Willie, while the others waited at the College gate.

"Helloa, yourself," answered Claude. "I hope you have made up your mind to go into training."

"I *am* in training," said Willie. "I have been preparing thith long time. I can run a hundred yardth in ten theconds."

"Oh, stuff!" said Claude.

"You mean you can tell a hundred lies in ten seconds," said Gerald, with refreshing frankness. "If you are in training, you shouldn't smoke."

"I don't!" cried Willie earnestly.

"Then the cigarette does," retorted Gerald.

"Thigarette!" cried Willie, with fine disdain upon his mobile face; "I wouldn't touch a thigarette with a ten-foot pole. The fellowth in Thaint Maureth never touch thigaretteth, and their team could play againtht your team here without the three backth and the quarterback and beat you thixty to nothing."

"If you're a specimen of St. Maure's, I don't want to go there," Gerald remarked.

"You wouldn't be able to thtand it," retorted Willie.

"All the same, Willie Hardy," said Claude, catching the boy's arm in a grasp which made Willie wince, "you must stop your cigarette smoking at once. As for training, your arm is as soft as a baby's and you can't stand an ordinary grip."

"When I wath at Thaint Maureth," returned Willie, "I had muthleth of brath."

"He means cheeks of brass," explained Gerald.

The party entered the college building in silence, Willie and Claude in the advance, while Gerald and Harry in their wake exchanged glances of mingled amusement and disgust.

Mr. Keenan was standing in the passageway. He beckoned to Harry.

"It's all arranged, Harry," he said. "I saw Father Trainer yesterday, and he expressed himself as being delighted to help a boy who is really in earnest about his mathematics."

"Thank you, Mr. Keenan. When shall I have a chance to see him?"

"There is a quarter of an hour yet before Mass. You might go up to him now. You will find his room on the third floor. It is the last but one to the left as you go down the corridor. Go to him at once; he wants to see you as soon as possible."

Harry ran upstairs two steps at a time, and Mr. Keenan turned away his head so as to escape seeing this breach of college discipline. The eager student reached the room somewhat out of breath and knocked timidly.

"Come in," said a strong, hearty voice.

Harry entered with alacrity, then paused and put on the face of astonishment.

There is a prejudice in the world at large to the effect that eminent scholars and eminent literary men are thin, bespectacled and venerable. Harry shared in this prejudice. On entering the room, this illusion received a shock.

The great mathematician was seated in a rocking chair; on his knees was a paper pad, in his hand a pencil, in his mouth a pipe at which he was pulling with no perceptible results. Though quite bald, he was not at all venerable. He was a stout, middle-sized man, with a round, ruddy, kindly face, upon which there was an expression of charming simplicity. There were no spectacles upon his nose, and his eyes, though they had just the least touch of introspection, were clear and bright. Had Harry met him on the street, it would never have occurred to him that he was passing an eminent thinker and a profound scholar.

"Good morning sir," said Harry, recovering from his astonishment.

"Good morning," returned the professor, rising with a smile, laying aside his pipe and, for some reason inscrutable to Harry, gazing at it mournfully. "Are you Harry Archer?"

"Yes, sir," said Harry, noticing as he spoke that the room was singularly destitute of books.

Father Trainer took up his pipe again.

"I'm glad to see you," he said. "By the way, you haven't a match about you, have you?"

"No, sir."

"My pipe is out. It is hard to get matches in this world."

"Excuse me one moment," said Harry, tripping from the room.

He returned very quickly with a handful of matches.

"Thank you very much."

Then the mathematician lighted his pipe.

"Well, Harry," he said with a smile, which was, as Harry styled it, 'jolly,' "are you really anxious to master geometry?"

"Indeed I am, sir. I am willing to let my sleep go, if necessary."

"Take a seat, Harry."

Harry took the only chair available in the room, for although there were two in addition to the rocking chair occupied by Father Trainer, one of these was heaped up with papers.

"What do you understand by an angle?" enquired Father Trainer.

Harry answered correctly.

The next question was an innocent one in all seeming and bore closely upon the definition of an angle. But before Harry had explained his answer, he found that he had practically gone through more than half of the first book in Wentworth's *Geometry*. On answering fully the third leading question, he discovered that he had finished the book. He was done with the entire second book within seven minutes from his entrance; and before the bell rang for Mass, Father Trainer had let his pipe go out several times, and Harry had to his own amazement told practically almost everything that he knew about geometry.

"Do you see any tobacco in the room?" asked the mathematician, when the boy had answered his last question.

"There it is behind you, sir," and Harry, as he spoke, arose, secured the box and handed it to Father Trainer.

"Ah, thank you! I had forgotten where I put it. That was the bell for class, was it? Well, Harry, I am more than pleased; I am delighted. You have talent for mathematics far above the ordinary. You may come to me for instructions anytime from two to six on Thursdays, and at six on Tuesdays and Saturdays. I haven't the least doubt but that you will make wonderful strides, for you have the mathematical turn of mind."

Harry, when he stepped out into the corridor, was blushing like a rose in June.

"Say," he said to Claude Lightfoot, as he took his place beside him in the ranks, "I have just met the greatest mathematician alive; and he's just as warm-hearted as if he didn't know any mathematics at all."

"You mean Father Trainer?" asked Claude.

"Yes."

"He doesn't look one bit like a mathematician—at least like the professors of science we read of in books," asserted Claude.

"That's so," said Harry heartily. "The only thing in him that reminds one of the scientific fellows in the storybooks is that he's a little absent-minded. He couldn't find his tobacco, although it was almost under his nose; and then he wanted matches, and when I got them I noticed a whole box of matches at the corner of his table under a sheet of paper. But just think! He's a warm-hearted man. Why, while I was answering his questions in mathematics, he was just beaming on me. And his voice was very kind and sympathetic."

"What was he asking you about mathematics for?" asked Claude.

Harry explained.

"Good luck to you, old boy. I was thinking of going in for that prize myself, but you will represent the College better than I could. And besides, as I'm captain of the eleven and want to try hard at verse writing, I'll have to let something go. I'll tell you what, Harry; I'll write to my sister at the Visitation Convent in St. Louis and get her to pray for you. She's just a stunner at praying, Kate is; and if you don't win that eighty dollars, it's because the Lord intended to give you something better."

Claude paused a moment.

"Is he really a good mathematician?" he said at length.

"Wonderful!" answered Harry. "I thought I knew something about mathematics, but he turned me inside out in ten minutes. And what is more, I learned from his questions."

"That's funny," said Claude. "I thought all great mathematicians were cross and dried up."

"So did I till just now, too," said Harry.

They then proceeded toward the College chapel, both of them, let us hope, relieved of one of the prejudices which nearly all the fiction of the day touching on the subject of savants has most industriously fostered.

Chapter VII

*IN WHICH IT IS SHOWN THAT FOOTBALL MAY BE A
HELP BOTH TO STUDY AND TO DEVOTION*

"LOOK here, Claude," said Harry, taking the captain of the football team aside, "why couldn't you play quarterback yourself? You can make a long pass as well as any player I ever saw."

"I learned it from you last year," said Claude. "If I felt quite sure that there was no hope of having you, I think I should take the position. Desmond is a good tackler and a fair kicker, and he might be put at fullback."

"Yes, he's not quite fast enough for a quarter; whereas, you can manage to be in pretty much every play, if you take the position."

"And besides," added Claude, "the quarterback's position is a good place for calling out the signals, and so if I were there I should be in a better position to captain the eleven than if I were playing fullback. I think I will follow your advice."

The classes had been dismissed just a few minutes before, and the football eleven were hard at it passing the ball.

"That will do!" cried Claude to the team.

"We shall now practice at passing the ball to the men when they are on the run. I shall act as quarterback. Maurice Desmond, for the present, at least, may practice for full-back. Now, give me the ball, and get back from me about five yards and two yards to my left. Each one of you will catch the ball as you are running at your full speed; the backs first, and the rushers beginning with the right and left end next. As each one catches the ball, he will return it to me on the run."

In the first trial, eight of the ten players dropped the ball, and five started too slowly. In the second trial, the result was more successful. For fifteen minutes did Claude keep them at this work, and when he called time, every player except Hardy had shown marked improvement.

In the next exercise, one player as before started at full speed and caught the ball from Claude, while two others ran closely behind. If the runner failed to catch it, it was the duty of one or the other who followed to fall upon it. In case the runner held the ball, the two were to follow him up until, at some point within his own discretion, he was to let it slip from his grasp, whereupon the follower nearest the fallen ball was to secure it at once.

There were more failures in this than in the preceding exercise, and it was continued for ten minutes.

"We shall have to practice that again," said Claude. "There seem to be only two players in the team who know how to fall upon the ball."

"Falling on the ball is not quite so easy as falling off a log," observed Gerald O'Rourke demurely.

"When I wath at Thaint Maureth," Willie remarked, "there wathn't a thingle player who couldn't do it every time; and we never lotht a ball on a fumble the whole time I wath there."

"Why didn't some of those famous St. Maure's players fall on Willie?" whispered Gerald to Maurice.

"There are but five minutes left, boys," continued the captain. "And we might as well take them out on an easy run around the yard. Line up quick."

On this their second run, they took a somewhat speedier gait than on the first occasion and made the rounds of the yard twice. Willie Hardy was puffing very hard at the end, and two or three others were slightly winded. Claude, nevertheless, was quite satisfied.

After practice, he called together the team in the gymnasium.

"This isn't exactly a football meeting," he began. "You know, boys, I am a Promoter of the League of the Sacred Heart, and all you fellows of Poetry class happen to be in my band. Now I think we might make work for the League and work for the eleven go together."

"That's right," said good-natured Charlie Pierson.

"They do something like that at Holy Cross College at Worcester, I believe," put in Gerald O'Rourke. "I have been told that the boys engaged or interested in athletics there have given a fine statue of the Sacred Heart to the College, and all through the season keep a light burning constantly before it. Shall we do something in that style? I'm sure we are all willing to chip in."

"When I wath at Thaint Maureth," put in Willie, just as Claude was about to speak, "the boyth uthed to play while wearing the badge of the League on their breathts."

"Didn't they wear their scapulars over their football suits and carry their beads in their hands?" asked Dockery.

Willie was about to lie again when Claude interposed.

"Score another for St. Maure's!" he said. "Well, boys, what I want to suggest is something which Mr. Keenan put into my head yesterday, and I think it a splendid idea."

Claude in his own way repeated the substance of his conversation with the prefect and ended by proposing that each player, besides making the usual morning offering, should also dedicate in a special manner the trials of training, the sacrifices, the hurts and the labors connected with football to the Sacred Heart.

"That's a first-rate idea!" said Drew. "I'm sure if I keep it in mind, it will help me to do better than I would otherwise."

"Why, it will help any fellow," added Stein. "If we all of us keep from smoking and eating between meals, and drinking water whenever we feel like it, we shall be living a pretty strict life."

"And you forgot about going to bed early and rising in good time," added Pierson. "I know, speaking for myself, that I hate to go to bed and won't go to bed till I have to, and that once I'm there, it's just the other way—I hate to get up and won't get up till I have to. I'm going to make a regular martyr of myself."

"And I say, Pierson," said Desmond with

a grin, "how about your going out visiting one night, and to the theatre another, and so forth?"

Pierson blushed as the whole crowd turned upon him their laughing eyes.

"I move," cried Dockery, rising, "that Pierson be forced to pledge himself not to go out to parties, visits, shows and the like from now till Thanksgiving."

"Oh, I say!" cried Pierson, "if you fellows will all agree to stay at home nights, I'll agree, too. That will be a new sacrifice, and while we're going about it, we might as well do the thing brown."

"I'll agree," said Willie, "and today I gave a five-pound bockth of candy to our thervant girl."

"It's a wonder you didn't give her your cigarettes, too," said Dockery; and he added gravely, "In fact, I think I have hit upon the right way of solving the servant girl question. Give her the deadly cigarette, and soon there will be no question because there will be no girl. But excuse me, I digress. Gentlemen, I agree with Hardy and Pierson. From now till December, any person who calls at my house anytime after seven o'clock in the evening will find me at home and attending strictly to business."

In brief, all agreed to this proposal with the single exception of Ernest Snowden.

Willie Hardy, the first to promise, went out that very night and satisfied himself by close examination that Lightfoot, O'Rourke and Desmond were staying within doors. Time and distance did not allow him to make a similar personal examination into the affairs of the other players. Let us hope that Willie returned to his home with strengthened confidence in boy nature.

On the same afternoon, as Mr. Keenan entered the College chapel to make a visit, he noticed the brother sacristan standing before the League intention sheet, with no little perplexity on his honest face.

"Look at this," whispered the brother; "some light-headed youngster has been marking acts of self-denial and mortification right and left. I should like to catch him." And he pointed to that part of the large blank sheet under the captions, "Acts of Self-Denial" and "Acts of Mortification."

Mr. Keenan looked and saw the following:

Self-denial: 1, 1, 3, 5, 3, 8, 7, 9, 3, 6, 8, 7, 6, 5, 7.

Mortifications: 1, 1, 1, 2, 2, 3, 1, 4, 3, 5, 4, 3, 2, 6, 3.

"That's absurd," said the brother.

"No, I think it's all right. Those numbers in lead pencil are made by different hands; and what's more, I think I know whose hands they are."

And Mr. Keenan knelt down to pray with something like a smile on his face, for the League and the eleven were both flourishing.

While Mr. Keenan was thus praying, Harry Archer was going his rounds for the first time. A skinny little boy, with very long legs and very short knee breeches, was guiding him.

Truth compels me to say that Harry looked shamefaced. Six months before, he had been something of an aristocrat. He had dressed stylishly and was even given to parting his hair in the middle on special occasions. And now, with a large bundle of papers, he was walking up the avenue in all humility where he had not infrequently paraded in youthful pride.

He glanced at the people he met on the avenue nervously and wondered whether they were looking at him in scorn. At Sixteenth Street and Fond du Lac Avenue he came upon Lambert Whistler, one of his former cronies.

Whistler stared at him in undisguised astonishment and, planting himself squarely in Harry's path, allowed a smile of scorn to mar the regularity of his soft, chubby features. Harry's blood boiled with shame and anger. Without asking an explanation of his whilom friend, he took Whistler's arm in a vice-like grip and with one strong jerk sent him reeling into the gutter. Then Harry, who had acted on impulse, recovered himself.

"I beg your pardon," he said, turning to the astonished Whistler.

Whistler took one look at the robust young paper carrier and concluded, very wisely, not to resent the indignity in kind. He bobbed his head in silence and went on.

"There's another friend gone," thought poor Harry. "I'll try to behave better after this." And so for the rest of the route he was more humble and more manly.

Harry was now learning lessons of patience and self-control of a nature which could not be learned even on the football field.

Chapter VIII

*IN WHICH NEW TROUBLES VISIT
THE ARCHER FAMILY*

"O Mother!" cried Harry one week later, "I can just tell you, I'm learning geometry. Father Trainer is something extraordinary! He simply gobbles up mathematics."

Mrs. Archer, who had been making a copy of a document, laid down her pen.

"What do you mean by his gobbling up mathematics, my dear?"

"Why, he takes up a book on Calculus or Quaternions and reads it through the same way as another man would a novel. He got a book of—Clerk-Maxwell's, I think it was—yesterday, and he stayed up last night till twelve, he told me. Though he went through it twice already when he was at his studies, he can hardly lay it down. This afternoon he put me through a whole book of geometry, one of the last in Wentworth's, and he made it as plain as daylight. Most of the book I had never studied before. And whenever I see a hard point, he looks so happy and pleased and lets his pipe go out and loses his matches. He's the most affectionate man I ever met. And Mother, I've got to like him so well that today I told him our story. He's the first man I've had the courage to tell it to, and he was so interested. He got very excited when I told him I was working for that eighty-dollar prize because we needed the money, and said that if I didn't win it, he'd give up the study of mathematics for the rest of his life. Why, he's just sure that I'll win."

"Perhaps he talks in that strain to give you courage, Harry," suggested the mother.

"No, I think not. I don't know why it is, but he really has the greatest confidence in me; and when a man likes me and has confidence in me, it puts me on my mettle and makes me work. Now I really think that if I were to lose the prize I should feel as bad about Father Trainer's disappointment as about losing the honor and the money."

"And that's why you stay up at your books every night till I force you to bed?" said Mrs. Archer with a smile.

"It's one reason, Mother; but besides, I naturally love mathematics, and the more I study it, the more I love it; and then Father Trainer has got something of his own enthusiasm into me."

"And how about your other studies, my dear?"

"Oh, I give them enough time to keep up with the other fellows. I'm no good at all in verse and English composition. That, I suppose, is because I have no imagination. At least I thought so till lately. But Father Trainer says that any boy with a really good head for mathematics has generally a good imagination, too, if he only knew how to wake it up."

"I say, Harry!" cried Paul, bursting into the room like a small cyclone and almost upsetting his mother by the affectionate dash which he made at her; "I say, Mama, I've got a job too!"

Harry reached over a powerful hand, caught his brother by the collar and lifted him wriggling into the air.

"Well, youngster, if you promise to be quiet and to tell us about your job, I'll let you down."

Master Paul, who had great respect for the vice-like grip of his brother, promised readily.

"I'm a carrier for the *Evening Journal*, and I got the position all by myself, and it's one dollar and a quarter a week. Harry, I'm going to buy you a bicycle the first thing, then next I'll buy Alice one, or maybe I'll buy one for myself before I get Alice hers.

Girls don't need bicycles, anyhow."

"Here's Alice now," said the mother.

A light step upon the stairway and a sweet alto voice caroling forth a cheerful air were heard, and with a smile which simply radiated good humor, Alice entered. She kissed her mother and Paul, gave Harry a saucy slap and said:

"I really do love to go out and give lessons because it's such a pleasure to get home again. With one mother and two brothers to cheer me up, I forget all my cares."

Whereat Paul and Harry and Mrs. Archer laughed heartily, for if Alice ever had experienced a care, she had kept it very successfully to herself.

In appearance, Alice was very like Harry. She was of somewhat darker complexion, and of regular features. Although, as was not the case with her brother, she was rather slender, the gracefulness and quickness of her movements, the bright, merry flash of her eye, the animation which she displayed in conversation evinced that she shared with him his splendid health.

"Say, Alice, do you want a bike?" cried Paul.

"Not now, Paul. Have you one to sell?"

"I'm in business now," answered the little

man. "And if you need anything, just let me know."

"Think of it!" cried Harry; "this young gentleman of eight—"

"It's eight and a half," interpolated Paul.

"This young gentleman of eight and a half is actually engaged in commercial pursuits which bring him in the munificent income of one dollar and twenty-five cents a week."

"You don't say!" cried Alice, while little Paul swelled up with importance. "We'll have to get a carriage and four horses; and I might as well give up teaching little girls with flaxen curls to play on the piano. By the way, I lost one of my little white-headed darlings today."

Mrs. Archer's hands trembled, and one of them went up nervously to her mouth.

"Then you have only two left," she said, despite herself betraying her anxiety. "Whom did you lose, my dear?"

"Nellie Perkins, if you please. Oh, you should have seen the scene; it was as good as a play." Alice threw herself upon a chair, rested her hands upon her knees and leaned over after the manner of a storyteller who has come to the part where he narrates with perfect zest. "You see, Mother, when Mrs. Perkins engaged me for little Nellie, she thought we were fairly well off and treated my offering to teach Nellie almost as a personal favor. She told me not to bother about terms, that there would be no trouble about them whatever, and said she considered it an honor to have me teach her da-a-a-rling— that's the way she drew the word out."

"I suppose she thought you were teaching Nellie the piano for your health," observed Harry.

"Well, when I reached the house today, Mrs. Perkins walked into the parlor in this style." Here Alice stepped lightly over to the piano and played a few bars from Chopin's funeral march. "And her face," continued Alice serenely, "was like this." Alice produced a tuneful crescendo movement on the lower keys with here and there a tiny burst of sound from the treble.

"Hurrah!" cried Paul, "I see the point. She looked stormy—thunder and lightning."

"Exactly," cried Alice, allowing the rumbling to die away. "And then I knew that she had found me out, and I remembered that it was no harm to be poor unless one was discovered in the act, and so I became desperate and carried myself thus"—Alice's nimble fingers executed one of Mozart's stately minuets, while Paul, puffing out his breast and his cheeks, marched sedate and stately about the parlor with his thumbs stuck through an imaginary pair of suspenders. "Mrs. Perkins wanted to know my terms, as she desired, so she said, to conduct matters with me on strict business principles; and I said twelve dollars a quarter, with ten weeks to the quarter. And becoming just the least little bit sarcastic when I saw this look on her face"—here Alice's hand came down in a crashing discord—"I added that my terms were strictly in advance, but that knowing her high business integrity I was willing to waive a point and trust her until the quarter was expired. Then Mrs. Perkins said that she could not possibly pay me such an extravagant sum when she could easily get a *man* teacher for the same rates. No wonder," continued Alice, going off into a minor key and putting something of a wail into her voice, "no wonder that we women have no chance compared with men, when the Mrs. Perkinses of the world act thus. Such things as this tempt me to become a new woman [feminist], and I should yield, too, were it not for the fact that most of the new women of my acquaintance happen to be old women, too."

"That's right," said Harry cheerfully. "But tell us what you did."

"I'm afraid I lost something of that gravity which I was resolved to keep. In fact, I talked this way." Alice was now performing an Irish jig. "And it all ended with my getting six dollars for five weeks' lessons. I am afraid that my pride got the better of me, too, for on receiving the money, I said that I was thinking of asking her for a 'character.' And then you should have seen her face. I couldn't play anything like it on the piano. Would you really believe it, she was about to refuse me a 'character' when I interrupted her with, 'But, Mrs. Perkins, I fear that my short apprenticeship at teaching your child will hardly justify me in asking you so great a favor. Good day.' Of course Mrs. Perkins, who is almost absolutely insensible to sarcasm, tried to look intelligent; and you know how people look when they try to look intelligent and don't know what they're expected to be intelligent about. I left her that way and departed at a"—Alice's fingers supplied the word "gallop."

"My child," said Mrs. Archer, "I'm afraid you were a little impudent. Remember that Mrs. Perkins is a lady."

"At least there's a popular prejudice to that effect," supplemented Harry.

"And besides," added the mother gently,

"she is your senior. We must all of us be respectful to our elders."

"You are right, you dear Mama. I preach that kind of doctrine myself, and I try to practice it. But you see, I'm not used to being poor, and I get taken unawares in my poverty. But really I am sorry for that speech about 'character' and for admitting that I was willing to trust her, but, Mama, she was really so aggravating. And besides," added Alice with a laugh, "she is not quite sure whether I was serious or not, so if I were to apologize, she would then know for certain that I had been facetious at her expense."

"I say, Alice, where's that money?" asked Paul.

"Here, little candy-destroyer, in my pocket. And as you're such a delightfully good little boy, I'll give you ten cents of it, and the rest goes to your poor mama."

Paul vanished. Whenever this young gentleman came upon a nickel or a dime, he invariably disappeared from the house and, having graced the neighboring candy shop with his presence, would return after a reasonable interval with fingers that were sticky and manifest anxiety about the time of the next meal.

Harry then narrated for the first time how

his pride had got the better of him in the encounter with young Whistler.

"You were worse than I, Harry," laughed Alice.

"Yes, but I recovered myself at once and apologized."

"Both of you, my dears," said the good mother, whose face had lost its sadness as the brother and sister were thus turning their little trials into comedy; "both of you are learning the lesson which every American boy and girl ought to learn, that there's nothing to be ashamed of in honest poverty. If you were not ashamed, you would both have restrained yourselves better."

"That's right, Mother," said Harry. "And now I'm going off to my mathematics."

Mrs. Archer and Alice then fell into a discussion of ways and means. If anything, the future had grown darker since the opening of our story. The water-rates man had come, and the taxes had been met, and now there were but fifteen of Harry's forty dollars left. While they were speaking, there was a ring at the doorbell.

Mrs. Archer started.

"It's a collector, Alice!" she exclaimed with a sad smile. "I know it is; I can tell by the way he rings; and of course, it's some bill that we know nothing about. Your poor father used to settle these things himself and, so far as can be found out, kept no record of trifling bills."

"Let me go down, Mother," said Alice. "You have to face that kind of trouble enough when I am out."

With a gesture, Mrs. Archer restrained Alice and hurried down the stairs. She looked very timid indeed, as she threw open the door to a small young man with a fierce moustache and a billious complexion. The stranger noticed her timidity and looked fiercer than ever. He was one of nature's bullies.

"This Mrs. Archer's house?"

"Yes; please step into the parlor."

The man followed Mrs. Archer, who carefully closed the door. She did not wish her children to hear the dialogue, for, good mother that she was, she chose to suffer alone.

"I have come," said he of the fierce moustache in a loud, harsh voice, "about this here bill of fourteen dollars from the firm of Haberdasher & Crash, and I'd like to get the money at once. It's due for four months."

"Please to talk in a lower tone, sir," said Mrs. Archer. "There are others in the house."

The little collector drew himself up till he

must have fancied himself six feet in height, while Mrs. Archer read the itemized bill.

"Well," she said at length, "I must say that I knew nothing about this debt till just now."

"Oh, of course!" said the man mockingly.

"And I should prefer examining into the matter before paying, to see that there is no mistake."

"Look here, Madam!" cried the collector in a hard, dictatorial voice, "I want you to understand that our firm isn't in the habit—"

"Not so loud, please."

"Isn't in the habit of making mistakes." His voice, despite the warning and Mrs. Archer's pitiful face of appeal, grew louder. "And besides, Madam, we are not in the habit of waiting from four to five months for our payments. We pay promptly and we expect our customers to do the same. You talk calmly of making us wait a little longer till you have the leisure to examine into that there bill. You have had four months to look into that little matter; and I want you to understand, Madam, that that kind of an excuse don't go down with a man of my experience. I reckon I know the time of day and I'm too old a bird to be caught with that sort of chaff. The fact of the matter is that you want to dodge paying this bill, and—"

"Excuse me, Mother," came a voice from the hall, as the parlor door was thrown open, "but has that man come about a bill against my father?"

Harry was standing in the doorway, and his mother could see that, despite his apparent calm, he was holding himself in by heroic efforts.

"Yes, Harry."

"Will you please step out here, sir," he said with an air of authority. "Mother, kindly wait where you are for a moment."

The collector had no sooner come into the hallway than Harry closed the door tight and caught his arm in a grip which caused the fierce young man to shrivel up. As Harry would say, he "had not played football for nothing." On clasping the arm, he flashed such a look into the man's face that the fierce moustache actually seemed to droop.

"See here," said Harry in a low whisper; "the lady you spoke to just now is my mother. As she is a lady, she is accustomed to deal with gentlemen. I am sure that you didn't realize that fact just now. Suppose, now, you step back into the parlor and tell her that you are sorry for your rudeness."

The man hesitated; he ended his hesitation with a groan, for Harry's fingers had closed upon his puny arm with terrific force.

"Madam," he said as he was ushered into the parlor under the same grip, "I take back what I said. I am sorry."

Harry then led him to the door.

"Are there any other collectors for your firm?"

"No."

"That's too bad. Anyhow, it won't do for you to come back here. If the bill is all right, we shall call and pay it within a week. But if your firm insists on sending a collector here, let them send someone else. For if you dare show your face here again, I shall help you out of this hallway and down these steps on sight."

Then Harry shut the door in the bully's face.

"Well, Mother, I think I was right this time. No man shall talk that way to my mother or sister if I can help it. But I'm mighty glad I didn't strike him."

He brightened as he added, "But I'll wager anything that he'll have a beautiful blue mark around his arm for the next ten days."

Mrs. Archer kissed her boy.

"Indeed, Harry, you are the man of the family."

Alice joined them, and after going over

the occurrence, it was decided at the earnest instance of Alice and Harry that henceforth all collectors with their bills should be referred to the man of the family.

Chapter IX

IN WHICH HARRY BEGINS TO SUSPECT THAT HE IS BURNING THE CANDLE AT BOTH ENDS

ON the second day of November, the students of Milwaukee College assembled in their hall to attend to what is called "the reading of notes."

After the leaders of the various classes had been publicly announced by the vice president and badges given to those who excelled in the several branches, the members of each division returned to their proper room to receive from the hands of their teachers testimonials of excellent deportment.

Mr. Keenan, as he faced his pupils, was evidently in great good humor.

"Boys," he said, "I congratulate you on your splendid record. You are all on the good conduct list, and with one exception, all of you have made over eighty-five merit marks out of a possible hundred in your competitions."

Willie Hardy, it may be observed, was the one shining exception. He was credited with but sixty-nine merit marks, several of which he had earned by an earnest but furtive perusal of Claude Lightfoot's paper in mathematics. Willie was blessed with good eyes.

"We'll do better still for the Christmas reading of notes," said Dan Dockery enthusiastically.

"Do you notice, Mr. Keenan," said Gerald O'Rourke, "that all the football players in the class have over ninety notes?"

"All except Willie Hardy," corrected Maurice Desmond.

"Do you mean to say," put in Dockery disdainfully, "that Willie is a football player?"

"I wath thuffering from headacths all lath month," said Willie.

"Why don't you drop your cigarettes, then?" asked Harry Archer, looking severely at Willie. "You're the only boy on the eleven who isn't in training. If you go on the way you're going now, you'll be a mark for any team we meet."

"You're jealouth," said Willie.

As the reader will perceive, this was an informal gathering of the class.

"Suppose we change the subject," said Mr. Keenan with a laugh. "Instead of criticizing what is wrong, we might praise what is right. Now let us take Charlie Pierson. Last year his record was rather poor. He just succeeded in passing the examinations in the class of Humanities, and now he is up with Claude Lightfoot, Harry Archer, Gerald O'Rourke and Dan Dockery."

Charlie Pierson buried his face in his hands; but even then one could see the deep blush which, overspreading his features, had carried its telltale signal behind his ears. The football players almost to a man were laughing delightedly.

"I think it would be no harm to give Charlie away," said Gerald, with a giggle.

"Shut up, will you?" said Charlie, raising his head, and having delivered this bit of advice, lowering it again.

"No, I won't," replied O'Rourke. "The fact is, Mr. Keenan, that last year Charlie was a sort of a ladies' man."

Pierson raised his head and gazed fiercely at Gerald. There was another roar of laughter from the class, in which Mr. Keenan joined, while Charlie effaced himself again.

"And," continued Gerald undauntedly, "he was either going to parties or getting up parties. It was a sort of an ice-cream-and-lemonade life. Several of the College boys were in it, but none of them seemed to get along well in class."

"Mr. Keenan!" cried Claude, jumping from his seat and incidentally so striking Willie Hardy with his elbow as to damage a package of cigarettes, much to Willie's subsequent distress, "did you ever know of a college boy who was what they call a ladies' man getting on in his studies?"

"No," said Mr. Keenan decidedly. "And what is more, I never expect to. Boys of that kind dress well, know how to talk nicely, to enter a room and leave it gracefully, but they are almost invariably shallowpates. I had rather be an awkward, rough youngster with ideas, than a smooth, smiling dandy without. It is easy for a man with brains to acquire polish, but almost impossible for a ladies' man of the kind we speak of to acquire ideas. And besides, any boy who has a good home may learn his manners there."

"That's so," said Claude heartily.

"And on the other hand," continued the teacher, "I have found it quite common to see the leaders of athletics also the leaders in studies. At St. Maure's, for instance, I was personally acquainted with the football players and baseball players of the first teams. Of the eleven football players, the six best, with one exception, were leaders in their classes. The one exception was notoriously a ladies' man. Of the baseball players, three out of five were leaders in their classes, the fourth was the same ladies' man, and the fifth I couldn't account for, as I knew nothing of his antecedents."

"When I wath at Thaint Maureth," began Willie—at this point he turned around to remonstrate with someone who had pinched him.

"But, Mr. Keenan," objected Gerald O'Rourke, ignoring Willie, "last year the boy who took the gold medal in the graduating class was notoriously a ladies' man. How do you account for that?"

"Was he a ladies' man in the lower classes, Gerald?"

"No, sir; he began his ice-cream-and-lemonade life in Philosophy class."

"Oh, that explains it! Doubtless he had been a good student in the lower classes, and the impetus he had gained before reaching Philosophy carried him on. When I was speaking of such boys, I referred to those who begin social life early. It would be much better if students were to wait till they have taken their degrees before they attempt to dazzle society with their luster; still, if they do insist upon letting their light shine in the last year of the course, while they will at once lose in studies, they will not be able to undo utterly the manly, studious life of their first years at college."

Somebody whispered, "Snowden," and there was a titter. Mr. Keenan gave no sign that he had caught the name.

"I don't think that athletics need interfere with study," said O'Rourke.

"I know it," added Claude. "If a fellow doesn't tire himself out with games, he's in better condition for study than if he didn't play at all."

"That's a fact," assented Archer. "I find this year that whenever I get a good bit of exercise, I can do more study in two hours than I can on other days in three."

"All the same," objected Stein, "you're doing a great deal better this year than you did last year."

"That's because I stay in of nights. Last year I used to go out a great deal."

"That was Charlie Pearson's trouble too," said Dan Dockery wickedly.

"And I'm having more fun and more study this year," said Charlie.

"*Mens sana in corpore sano*," quoted the professor. "Now, Harry, as it's only half-past two, you might take a little exercise this afternoon with the players. You don't look well at all. There's quite a difference between you and the boys in training."

And so there was. Harry in the past two months had changed greatly. His cheeks had lost their flush of health, and there was a dark circle under his eyes which told of late hours and sedentary habits. Claude and Gerald and Dan and Charlie and Maurice, on the contrary, had succeeded in getting into what is called the pink of condition. Their training had been a training with Christian temperance for its groundwork. Avoiding tobacco, eating nothing between meals, abstaining from all stimulants, going to bed early and rising betimes, guarding against any excess even in physical exercise, they were leading lives in which nature and grace joined hands—lives of perfect purity and admirable self-restraint. With them a love for athletics and a love for the League of the Sacred Heart went hand in hand, and the natural was brought into close union, as doubtless God intended it, with the supernatural. Stein, too, was in fair condition; but Hardy looked as soft and as flabby as on the day of his entering the classroom. As for his complexion, it was becoming sallow. Despite his hardy constitution, the baneful, factory-made cigarette was beginning to do its work.

Fifteen minutes later, eleven young men, among them Harry Archer, issuing from the gymnasium, came out into the yard in full football suits.

"Halloa!" cried Claude with a shout of delight. "There's Frank Elmwood. Halloa, Frank! You're just the man we've been wanting to see."

"And you're just the men *I've* been wanting to see," rejoined Elmwood. "Go on, now, with your practice; I want to see what you can do."

Frank Elmwood had been graduated from Milwaukee College two years before; he had then gone to Georgetown University for a course in literature and, after carrying away all the honors within his reach, had returned to Milwaukee as local correspondent for a Chicago daily paper. Besides his reportorial work, Frank was so busily engaged in various literary labors and studies that he had thus far been unable to attend a single practice of the Milwaukee College team.

The eleven one by one shook hands with Elmwood, and then, at the bidding of their captain, fell into line, Harry Archer taking Claude's place as quarterback.

Standing beside Claude, Frank Elmwood watched each movement closely.

"My, but that Archer knows how to pass a ball!" said Frank. "It is no sooner snapped back than he has it ready for the man, but he doesn't seem to know the signals well."

"You see, Frank, he doesn't belong to the team this year!"

"What?" cried Frank, taking off his glasses.

"We can't get him to play. The Central High School eleven are jubilant over it and think they have a sure thing for Thanksgiving Day. And I'm afraid they have reason for thinking so. Still, if it were not for two positions we would have a magnificent team."

"And one of the positions, I can see," said Frank, "is pretty Willie Hardy, the left tackle. He's a perfect contrast to every other player on the team. The rest of them start off at the signal like a lot of minnows. In fact, if Hardy can hold his man, you fellows can never lose on hitting your opponents' line."

"Mr. Keenan deserves credit for their quickness in starting. Every night for a week, he had us all in line for a five-yard race. Of course, the winner of the five-yard race is practically the one who makes the quickest start. Now in the beginning of the practice it is a fact that the best runners made the best time. But as they went on practicing, the others got the trick of starting fast, and now if you stand our eleven on a line and send them off to the sound of one of our signals, it requires a good eye to pick out who are the laggards—excepting, of course, Hardy, who seems to have learned nothing of the trick."

"Who is the other player that you don't trust?"

"Ernest Snowden. He has been sullen all along, and although he is one of the best players, he doesn't seem to take any interest in the game. Besides, his wind is not very good. I am told that he doesn't keep our training rules. He smokes a good deal and eats and drinks when he feels like it and goes out a great deal at night. He wants to be considered in society. Last year he was our best man for hitting the line, and his best point is his weight. He is over one hundred and seventy-five pounds. I don't see how we can replace him; and yet, I'm afraid that he'll bring matters to a head some day in such a way that either he or I shall have to leave the team. Ever since I've been captain, he has made himself as disagreeable to me as possible."

"Have you no substitutes, Claude?"

"None that amount to anything. The only fellow in the College outside our eleven who really knows the game, and plays it pluckily, is George Hastings of the Junior team; but then he's so abominably light that he could hardly play with us. He's barely more than ninety-six or -seven pounds. There he stands just outside the green watching the fellows practice."

"Call him over here. We may use him."

"Say, George, come over this way!" cried Claude.

A handsome boy of sixteen, tall and slim, with a very regular, oval face, approached. He did not look at all strong, though there was a springiness in his movements which denoted quickness.

"Frank, this is George Hastings, fullback of our Junior football team."

"Glad to see you," said Frank. "I want you and Claude to help me give the eleven there a few lessons. You're not afraid, are you?"

George blushed, broke into a smile and said modestly:

"I think not, sir."

"Well, take off your coat and be ready to help. By the way, Claude, your players do not seem to know much about tackling a runner. They seem to think that the idea of tackling is to catch hold of the runner with the ball anyhow and anyway and hold on to him. That's not it at all. The man who tackles must, as a rule, tackle hard and low, so as to keep the runner from making any further gain. Claude, tell your players I wish to say something to them."

Claude made a sign, and the practice stopped.

"Boys," said Frank, "I want to congratulate you on your offensive play. In passing and receiving the ball, and starting off at full speed with every man in the line attending to his work and attending to it at once, your teamwork is simply wonderful. But what about your defensive play—your play, I mean, when the other side has the ball? Your tackling is simply infamous. So far, I have seen only one player who tackles correctly, and that player, unfortunately, does not belong to your team at all—I mean Harry Archer."

"What ith the matter with our tackling?" asked Willie.

"Too high and too gingerly," answered Elmwood.

"In St. Maureth," objected Hardy, "the fel-lowth were much better at football than they are here; and all of them uthed to tackle near the shoulderth, and they would pull the runner back from five to fifteen yardth."

This statement was received with great hilarity.

"Were you trained to tackle that way, Willie?" asked Frank.

"Yeth, I wath."

"Give me the ball," whispered Frank to Claude. "Now," he added aloud, "I'm going to stand fifteen yards from you, Hardy, and I'm going to run straight toward you with the ball. You may tackle me."

Frank put the ball under his left arm and started at an easy run toward Willie. The great left tackle of St. Maure's at once placed himself so as to face Frank's left. As Elmwood noticed this, he suddenly changed the ball from one arm to the other and, upon Willie's advancing to tackle him, swept him aside with a straight arm and continued unhindered down the field.

"That wath a trick!" cried Willie.

"It wath a joke," mimicked Dockery.

"Yes; but high tackling gives a chance for that kind of a trick," answered Frank. "Suppose you try it over. This time, I will not interfere with your attempt to tackle."

Taking the same position, Frank again came at a run toward Willie. Just before Hardy made to throw his arms about him, Frank put on all his speed. Willie held him, and the two went on together for more than five yards beyond the spot where Elmwood was tackled.

"Do you call that tackling?" asked Frank, picking himself up.

"What ith wrong about it? I brought you down."

Frank was too disgusted to reply.

"Here, Hastings," he said, "I want to speak to you a minute. Now," he whispered, "I want to shame these fellows into good tackling. If they see a little boy, or rather a boy your size and lightness doing it, they will all throw themselves into the work."

"I'll try to do anything you say," said Hastings.

"Very good; now first of all don't be afraid; secondly, make a dive at my legs just above the knees; and thirdly, dive hard."

"I think I can do all that, sir."

"I ask you because Claude tells me that you are fearless. Now, boys, George Hastings is going to tackle me. Stand there, George, where Hardy stood before."

With what looked like absolute fearless-
ness, Hastings, at the proper moment, made
a dive at Frank and downed him in his tracks.

Frank arose rubbing his shoulder.

"There," he said, "I didn't gain one inch.
I am one hundred and fifty-four pounds, and
a boy of less than one hundred holds me
fast. With good tackling the lightest player
can hold the heaviest, but with high tackling it becomes very often a question of brute
strength and weight."

Frank gave the ball to Claude and told
him to run full speed at Harry. Claude went
down quite suddenly. Several of the heavier
players then took the ball, and were tackled with the same result.

And now every boy on the team wanted
a chance to tackle. They were all aroused to
enthusiasm; and so great was the demand
for men to be tackled that several of the
heavier students not belonging to the eleven
were induced to run with an imaginary ball.
For half an hour, tackling went on fast and
furious; and the improvement within that
time was really remarkable. To Elmwood, a
most gratifying evidence of their training
was the fact that none of them became
winded. Hardy, it must be said, had retired
when the practice in tackling began on the

plea that his ankle was hurting him; and Snowden excused himself to Lightfoot, as he had to meet his mother "downtown" at exactly half-past three.

"How in the world, Claude, did you get your players to have such a command over their breathing?" asked Elmwood.

"In two ways, Frank. First, none of them smokes, nor eats between meals, and they keep good hours; secondly, I have followed a sort of practice which Mr. Keenan suggested, and it has worked like a charm. If you wish I'll show it to you."

Claude clapped his hands, and with military-like precision, the rushers fell into line and the backs into their respective places.

"Tell them what you think of their tackling, Frank," whispered Claude.

"Just one word, boys. You have already improved very much in tackling, but there is room, plenty of it, for improvement. Some of you tackle as a timid man dives. Any of you who know anything about the water must know that it is the timid diver who gets the headache, who fails to cut the water nicely, whereas the bold diver meets with no inconvenience. It's the same way with tackling; tackle with confidence, and tackle hard. Remember that football is a rough game, but not a rude game. Hard tackling is perfectly proper; if possible, you should always force a man back a yard or two by your tackle. The general rule is to tackle low; but in case the runner is lighter than yourself, or in case, though heavy, he has not full speed on, it might be good to catch him high and force him back, even carry him back if you are able."

"That ith the way they uthed to do at St. Maureth," mimicked Dan Dockery.

"Supposing Willie to have spoken the truth," said Frank, "we may conclude that the St. Maure's eleven was much heavier than the opposing teams. Now, Claude, let's see how you train your men for keeping their wind."

Leaving the "green," the eleven ranged themselves in one line in the yard.

"Forward!" said Claude.

Keeping time, time, time in a step somewhat faster than marching, they advanced some twenty yards. Suddenly Claude gave a short, sharp cry, and at once the entire team started off as though they were engaged in a hundred-yard dash. They had scarcely made twenty-five yards when the same short, sharp cry was heard, and, not at once, but with astonishing quickness, the runners checked themselves and, hastening into line, again resumed their march.

"That is splendid!" said Frank to Mr. Keenan, who, as the reader may have observed, had effaced himself to all intents and purposes once the team had had their first few practices.

"Isn't it? Claude Lightfoot is a splendid trainer. Didn't you notice how fast those runners stopped themselves and got into line. If the two absentees, Hardy and Snowden, were at all like the ones practicing now, I should allow the team to play a game with some outside eleven next week. But as it is, I think it better to play no game till Thanksgiving, when we meet the Centrals."

"That is safest, since you have practically no substitutes," said Elmwood. "You will need every man to be at his best on that day. The Central High School have a strong eleven this year. They play like tigers—gentlemanly tigers, that is, and haven't been scored against in the three games they have played."

"Lightfoot tells me that they expect to beat us hands down."

"So I have heard. Halloa, there they are running again! That's fine; they keep together pretty well. With some improvement in their tackling, I think they will hold their own against the Centrals, who on account of

Archer's not being in our team, and Hardy's being in it, think they are going to have a snap. Ah, they have run about fifty yards, and now they are walking again!"

"You see the idea, don't you? They are training in one and the same exercise for short runs and long runs, and for falling into line with the utmost dispatch. Halloa! Archer has dropped out."

Harry approached them as Mr. Keenan was speaking, looking rather pale and breathing heavily.

"You're not in condition, old boy," cried Frank.

"I—I guess not," panted Harry, "and if I don't stop now and take a rest, I shall be too dead tired to carry my papers. Goodness, how I've changed! This time last year, I hardly knew what it was to be tired."

"What time do you go to bed, Harry?" asked Frank.

"Oh, eleven or twelve o'clock. You needn't make such eyes at me. I can stand it. In fact, I don't feel sleepy any more, and sometimes I lie awake an hour or so longer.

Mr. Keenan, as he listened, became very grave.

"Harry," he said, "I'm afraid you are hurting yourself. You are studying hard and playing little. 'All work and no play,' you know, 'makes Jack a dull boy.' Even Father Trainer is getting frightened."

"Yes; he wants me to stop studying mathematics and says that it will be enough if I just work two or three times a week with him."

"And aren't you going to do it?"

"Well, sir, I'd like to think first. You see, I want to win that prize; and I know that Father Trainer would be awfully disappointed if I didn't. And besides, I just love to go ahead with those problems. The more I work at them, the more I like them. Father Trainer told me once that in the study of mathematics there was a fascination frantic, and now I'm beginning to believe him."

"You had better believe him on the other point, too," counselled Frank, "or you'll find out that you have made a mistake."

"Perhaps you are right, Frank, and indeed I want to follow his advice; and yet, I can't bring myself to do it."

"I am sure your spirit of obedience will determine you," said Mr. Keenan kindly.

After supper that evening Harry went to his books as usual. But he lacked his customary serenity of mind. He felt gloomy and disturbed. Matters had not gone well of late with the little household. They were within one month of the time when the interest on the mortgage fell due, and beyond the odd small change for trifling expenses, Mrs. Archer had but twenty-five dollars on hand.

With strict economy the sum might be brought up to forty, and one hundred and five dollars were needed. If he could but win the eighty-dollar prize all would be well; five or ten dollars more could be got together in some way or other. But to give up study, Harry reasoned, was practically to give up the eighty dollars. On the other side, to continue applying himself until late at night was to go against the advice of mother, of sister, of Father Trainer, of Mr. Keenan.

Poor Harry was in a quandary as he sat at his desk. He was so absorbed that he failed to notice the entrance of Alice till she touched his shoulder with her hand.

"What do you want?" he cried brusquely and with a sudden start.

Alice drew back as though she had received a blow.

"Oh, I beg your pardon, Alice!" he said in dismay. "I don't know what's the matter with me. I didn't know I had spoken till the words were out of my mouth. Please don't mind me, Alice, for acting like a bear. I'm cross and troubled, and feel so mean."

Harry's head drooped, and the girl gazing at him in loving pity was touched almost to tears.

"My poor brother," she said. For a moment she could not go on. "Harry, you are not well. You are killing yourself with your regular studies and with working for that prize. Now, Harry, you've got to let the mathematics go."

"But I can't, Alice; I want to make our mother happy by winning that prize. She'll be proud of me, and she'll be able to keep our home. Really, I can't give up. Indeed, I don't feel quite as well as I ought to, but I'll take the risk and keep on till November the thirtieth.

"Very well," said Alice. "Then tomorrow I will sell my piano."

"Indeed, you won't," cried Harry, starting to his feet.

"But I will and I shall. Unless you promise me here and now to give up your extra studies at home, I'll sell the piano tomorrow. I can get two hundred and fifty dollars for it."

"But how will you get on without a piano?"

"And how," said Alice, losing all control of herself, "shall mother and I get on without you?"

Here Alice, that jolly sister who was a

sunbeam day in and day out, began, despite her struggles to restrain herself, to cry.

I never yet knew a generous, noble-hearted boy who could withstand the tears of a mother or of a sister or, indeed, of any good woman. The tears were a stronger argument than the piano. Harry surrendered unconditionally.

Alice kissed him and hurried away. She was ashamed of her burst of emotion.

He went to bed early—before ten o'clock— and fell asleep presently, only to be aroused by a sharp, jerking sensation in the knee. He dozed off again, to be awakened a moment later by a similar jerk. Then he lay awake, and despite himself, his mind was hard at it solving certain problems which he had gone over with Father Trainer the day before. He heard the clock strike ten, then eleven, then twelve. A little before one, he fell asleep—but his sleep was by no means dreamless. Now he was engaged in the mathematical contest trying in vain to prove the simple proposition that the angles of a triangle were equal to two right angles; now he was trying to guard a man up the field, or attempting unsuccessfully to tackle a runner. His dream became a nightmare when he imagined himself to be crossing the "Jackasses' Bridge" on a bicycle.

He arose cloudy and bewildered at seven

o'clock. His eyes were heavy and his limbs stiff.

Little did Harry fancy that by his present mode of living he was actually courting a broken constitution for life.

Chapter X

IN WHICH HARRY AND CLAUDE TAKE A DRIVE

IT was nearing six o'clock on the following afternoon when a buggy drove up before Harry's home, and Claude, the sunny-faced, thoughtfully ignoring the step provided for the purpose of alighting, leaped down to the pavement.

"How do you do, Mrs. Archer?" he said, as she answered the bell, "I've come for Harry. All the fellows have been remarking how he's getting to be a regular hermit. He needs a touching up. Won't you please let me take him home to supper? Dan Dockery and Gerald O'Rourke are to be there, not to speak of other good fellows. I'll bring him back before nine o'clock. I'm sure it will do him good."

"It is very nice of you to come for him, Claude."

"Not half as nice as it is for me to get him, Mrs. Archer. Harry was very popular last year, but now he's more popular than ever; and we boys don't get half enough of him. We're all of us just as anxious about his winning that prize as he is; but we don't want him to break down."

"Neither do we, Claude!" cried Alice as she came out from the parlor. "So you've noticed it, too? You Milwaukee College boys have good hearts. Of course, Harry will go with you. In fact, I've half a mind to join you myself."

"No ladies need apply," laughed Claude, as he caught Alice's hand in his.

Claude liked Alice, as indeed did everyone who knew her.

"All right, young man," retorted Alice. "You needn't expect to see me at your next football game."

"Indeed, I don't expect to see anyone," said Claude simply, "except my own team and the opposing eleven; and that will be enough for me. But I do hope you will come. I think it will be a great game. Halloa, Harry!" continued Claude as the man of the house came down the stairs, "I've come to fetch you over to supper with Gerald and Dan and Pierson and some of the other fellows."

"Oho!" cried Harry, "that's the way you are training, is it? I thought you had to stay at home after nightfall."

"Yes, but Mr. Keenan suggested a break, just for the sake of variety. Tomorrow is a holiday, and we're all to take a late sleep and have a practice game in the afternoon. Get your hat, and come on."

"I wish, Claude," said Mrs. Archer, as Harry ran up the stairs, "that you would come over and see my boy a little oftener. You are a dear friend of his."

"To tell you the truth, ma'am, I have wanted to come over; but Harry won't come to see me, and I can't get him to invite me here."

"The fact is," laughed Alice, "Harry is growing proud. If you boys tease him a little, it will do him good. There is no one at home to tease him. Mother is too good, and I'm too fond of him, and little Paul, who is in business on his own account, has no time for trifles."

"Don't you believe Alice!" cried Harry, as he joined them at the doorway.

"But I do believe her," protested Claude. "You're getting away from the boys too much, and it's telling on you. But you'll get a good dose of them this evening. Come on, now."

At a rattling gait, Claude drove south till they reached Grand Avenue. Then he turned east.

"Halloa, where are you going, Claude! You are driving away from your house."

"I want to take you for a ride on Prospect Avenue where you can inhale the lake breezes and get the freshest kind of air in the market. We'll not go home till you're hungry. My mother has promised to get up an extra supper, and I want you to have the full benefit of it. Have you been at Lake Park lately?"

"No, Claude; I hardly ever go out."

"Well, we'll drive out there and stretch our legs by taking a run about the grounds. And then if you don't feel hungry, we'll take another run. Halloa, Pierson!" cried Claude, a few minutes later.

They were nearing the bridge which, spanning the Milwaukee River, connects Grand Avenue with Wisconsin Street. Charlie Pierson, walking westward with bent head, raised his eyes.

"Halloa!" he said, and added as he recognized Harry, "I'm glad to see you out."

"Where are you going?" asked Claude, who

had driven his horse to the curbstone.

"Just taking a walk and meditating on my poem for Friday."

"Jump in here—there's room for three easily—and we'll help you meditate. There you are. Get up, Sally."

"I'm glad I caught you," continued Claude, as they went briskly along Wisconsin Street. "I was just going over to your house to bring you home for supper. You got my invitation, didn't you?"

"Yes; but I didn't intend starting till later."

"A little fresh air won't hurt you, Charlie; though you don't by any means need it as much as this dough-faced young—"

"Look!" broke in Harry, nudging Claude sharply. "See that stout, stocky young fellow passing Romadka's trunk store? That's the captain of the Central High School Eleven, Charlie Seawell."

"I met him the other day," said Claude, "and I was glad to find that he was a perfect gentleman. I know most of the players on his eleven, and they are all nice fellows. I felt a little bad, though, when I noticed how stout and strong he is; and then I felt ashamed of myself for feeling that way. Both of us have agreed to stand up for clean playing. I have promised him to take off any player on my team whom I catch playing 'dirty football,' and he has made me the same promise. He is a lover of football and sees quite plainly that the only hope for the future of the game lies in its being made essentially a gentleman's game."

"Look out for Hardy, then," said Pierson. "He is as treacherous as a cat. In some of our practices, I caught him tripping up men, even those who didn't have the ball; and when I said something to him about it, he asserted that all the players at St. Maure's played that game."

"I'm afraid he'll ruin St. Maure's reputation if people believe him," said Harry. "If I were President of that College, I would take him back for nothing, so as to keep him out of the way."

"I'm worrying a little about Hardy," mused Claude. "He's a poor player and a mean player. He's not in condition, and though he is obedient enough when I deal with him directly, he is different when away from me. If we lose the game with the Centrals, it will be Willie's fault."

"Couldn't you put Hastings in?" suggested Harry.

"Too light, I reckon," Pierson answered.

"And besides," added Claude, "there's

another objection. Even supposing Hastings could do as well as Hardy, and I should not be surprised at all if he could, there would be great danger of his getting hurt on account of his light weight and want of strength. He's growing fast and should not be allowed to play except with middle-sized fellows. So I don't intend to bring him into the game, unless someone is injured."

"That's right," said Harry. "So long as teams are evenly matched and play a fair game, there's no more risk of accident than in baseball."

"You left out one important condition, Harry," said Claude.

"What is that?"

"Training! No man can afford to enter into a game who is not in good physical condition. Most of the accidents in football are due to the fact that men undertake to play without previous preparation. Men do not ride in bicycle races or attempt the hundred-yard dash without training; and I don't see why boys should go into a contest where every nerve and muscle of the body is strained over and over, without being prepared."

"Excuse the interruption, Claude, but here's the place to get your poetry!" cried Pierson enthusiastically.

They had reached the foot of Wisconsin Street and were gazing out upon the most beautiful bay, probably, in the interior of the United States.

"It is beautiful," said Harry. "I'm afraid we Milwaukee people don't appreciate it as we should."

"Why, since we've come out, you've got to look fifty percent better, Harry!" exclaimed Claude. "Look at his face, Charlie."

"It's the bloom of youth—only a little faded," replied the good-natured center rush. "You ought to come into training with us, my boy."

"Indeed, I wish I could!" exclaimed Harry fervently. "If I had known how hard it would be for you to get up an eleven, I might have gone in anyhow. But I gave it up for the sake of my mother. She needs me, now that father is gone. And now that I have a news-paper district, I couldn't practice regularly anyhow. And so if I were to join the team, I should set a bad example to the other fel-lows by irregularity in coming to practice."

"Well," Claude suggested, "you might come around for the Thursday practices, just to give the fellows a few pointers. All of them know that you understand the game better than any boy at the College."

"Though I must say that I don't know the game better than you, still, if you wish, Claude, I'll be around whenever I have a chance."

"Get up!" said Claude in great glee.

He now began to see a way out of difficulties which had bidden fair to be insurmountable.

From that time till Thanksgiving Day, November the twenty-fifth, Claude took Harry out for a drive three or four times a week. It was almost the only relaxation which Harry allowed himself; for beyond a few practices on Thursday, his duties at home and his studies kept him very busy. It is true that he relaxed somewhat in his work in geometry; but for all that, under Father Trainer's enthusiastic direction he made wondrous strides and, despite his promise to Alice, frequently sat at his desk until very late.

Chapter XI

*IN WHICH THE MORNING OF THANKSGIVING DAY
REVEALS SERIOUS INTERNAL DISSENSIONS
IN THE FOOTBALL TEAM*

AT ten o'clock precisely, the football eleven of Milwaukee College filed into the gymnasium.

"Is everybody here?" cried Claude.

"Ernest Snowden hasn't shown up," answered O'Rourke. "He made an awful mouth yesterday when you told us to come here this morning."

"I think he wath out at a party latht night," volunteered Willie Hardy.

This statement was tacitly set down for a lie by everyone within earshot. As a matter of fact, gentle Willie had told the truth. He himself had attended a party with Snowden, and both of them had indulged in ice cream and cakes to an inordinate extent. Willie, on this occasion, had been particularly brilliant and had related several football feats performed at St. Maure's which would certainly have astonished the students of that classic institution. In nearly all these accounts, Willie was the hero; and certainly, as he told his feats, he was entitled to be called a great player.

Even Mr. Heffelfinger's record paled in the light of the lisper's achievements.

"But," objected Mandolin Merry, a young lady of fourteen, already, despite her tender years, moving in social circles, "I thought that football players ought to go into training."

"Ineckthperienthed playerth—yeth," said Willie, casting the full radiance of his big blue eyes upon the young miss. "But fellowth who are thtrong like mythelf and Erneth don't need to mind."

Young Snowden, who despite his occasional violations of training was really a fine football player, looked displeased. It pained him to be classed with Hardy.

"Do you think you will beat the Centrals?" continued Mandolin.

"I'm afraid not," said Snowden. "We haven't had a professional coach, whereas the Centrals have been under the direction of one of the best players that ever attended Madison University. Then our captain is no good. He's too light and too bossy. They shouldn't have chosen a young fellow like him for captain, anyhow. I can hardly stand the fellow's insufferable airs."

"Neither can I," chimed in Willie. "He ith alwayth after me for going out at night."

"He got after me, too," said Snowden, who was now enjoying his third dish of ice cream. "But I shut him up pretty quick. He knows now that there is one man in the team who is not afraid of him."

"I've a good nothyun," said Willie, "to give him a trounthing after the game."

"Oh, please don't, Willie!" cried the society young lady of fourteen, clasping her hands together and looking beseechingly into Willie's heroic face.

"Well, for your thake," answered Willie magnanimously, "I'll not do it. I shall control mythelf."

The two then made eyes at each other, and for the time being perfectly contented with themselves and the world, of which they reckoned themselves shining ornaments.

But really it is time to return to the eleven. Besides the regular players, Harry Archer and George Hastings were in attendance: Hastings as substitute and Archer as chief counselor.

"I suppose Ernest Snowden is taking advantage of the fact that there is no one to fill his place to do just what he pleases," grumbled Dockery.

"Yes," assented Claude, with the nearest thing to a sigh that could proceed from a boy of his sunny disposition. "I've had to swallow a lot of insolence from him. But what can I do? I asked Mr. Keenan about him several times, and he told me to follow my own judgment. But when you haven't a man to take his place, where does the judgment come in?"

"'Oh, the little less, and how much it is!'" cried that lover of Browning, Charlie Pierson. "Just for the want of a single player, our captain has to stand that fellow with his spite and vanity. They say that I'm good-natured, but I wouldn't have stood him half as long as you have."

"It has been hard," Claude admitted; "but I suppose I can hold out for twelve hours more. Anyhow, we mustn't be too hard on him. He doesn't see things our way; but that's no reason why we should accuse him of pride and vanity. Everything we have against him is connected with football. He's a good fellow in every other way. Provided he obeys the signals, we'll get along. All of you look in splendid trim, except Hardy. Young man, you were up late last night. You've yawned three distinct times since we've entered this room."

"Look at his eyes," said Dockery

"I fell athleep at eight o'clock," protested Willie. "And I thlept like an infant, and I never felt better thinth the day I wath born."

"And you never looked worse," added O'Rourke. "Here's a pointer for you, young man; the Centrals are going to play their game against *you* from the start. Some college boy must have let out the condition of our team and told them that you were the weakest man in our line. If you've been staying up and breaking all discipline, you will be at fault for our losing the game."

"In case he doesn't hold his man," put in Claude gloomily, "we shall have to call in Hastings for the second half. I shouldn't like to do that, George," he added, with a kindly look at that young player; "for although you are all right as fullback for the Junior eleven, you will have an ugly time facing their tackle and standing the rushes of their heavy halfbacks."

"I'll do my best if you need me," said Hastings modestly, "and I'll try not to be frightened."

"Oh, you have pluck enough!" added Harry Archer encouragingly; "and you can tackle as well as any boy on the team."

At this point Ernest Snowden entered. He had a lighted cigar in his mouth and looked belligerent.

"I just came in to say that I have business downtown and won't be free till three.

I'll take my football togs along and meet you on the grounds."

"Can't you wait till we have discussed certain points of the play?" asked Claude, despite himself, looking annoyed.

"No; I understand the game well enough."

Claude's face flushed, and his fingers worked uneasily. He paused to control himself, while Snowden puffed at his cigar and faced the players with a disdainful smile.

"At least you can come here at two and dress with the crowd and go out with them to the grounds in a body."

"I can, maybe; but I won't."

If Claude lost his temper, I certainly cannot blame him.

Every boy there was angry; Harry Archer, who loved Claude and despised a bully, was furious.

His face was white, his lips quivering as he stepped up to the captain and whispering hoarsely:

"Don't stand it, Claude! An angel wouldn't endure that kind of treatment."

"Well," said Claude in a voice grown hard with anger, "you'll *have* to come here at two o'clock. I insist on that point, and I think you might have the decency to take that cigar out of your mouth. Mr. Keenan takes it for granted that nothing of the kind is to take place in this room, so long as we players have the privilege of using it."

"You can tell Mr. Keenan on me if you wish, you old blab," retorted Snowden; "but you'll not bully me any longer. If you expect me to help your team out, you'll have to let me have my way today, by way of variety. You have bossed me long enough. I hold the last trump."

Snowden looked about him with an air of triumph. He felt that he was master of the situation.

Claude paused. What was he to do? To lose Ernest Snowden was practically to lose the game. To endure his insufferable airs was asking too much.

Harry Archer stepped forward.

"Put him off the team, Claude. I'll play with you, if it's the last game I ever play."

A yell of joy and triumph arose from the throats of the hitherto silent spectators. Snowden's look of insolence died away. He had felt sure that he was needed and was not prepared for Archer's offer. He was thinking of giving in, and hoping only for a graceful occasion to make his submission, when Claude said firmly:

"Ernest Snowden, you can go. I think we

boys would rather lose the game than win
with your help."

"Hurrah!" cried the boys again.

Snowden took his cigar out of his mouth
and gazed in extreme chagrin at Claude.
While he was thus gazing, Archer, who was
by far the angriest boy in the gymnasium,
stepped over and, plucking the stump from
Ernest's fingers, threw it out of the nearest
window.

"Excuse me for my rudeness," he said, looking Snowden straight in the eye, "but I don't
see any other way of settling the matter."

But the discomforted halfback was too
absorbed in other matters to resent Harry's
action.

"What!" he gasped. "You dare to put me
out of the team after I've played on it for
three years. I've been practicing for a month
and I've paid over two dollars into the trea-
sury for one thing or another."

"Has any fellow here fifty cents?" Claude
inquired.

Collins handed him the required sum at
once.

"Here," said Claude, adding to this sum a
dollar and fifty cents out of his vest pocket.
"Take your money and go."

"But I'll not go!" roared Snowden, dashing the money to the ground. "I belong to this team, and I'll play the game for all it's worth!"

Claude was getting cooler; it was an artificial coolness. Had he followed his feelings, he would have assaulted Snowden then and there.

"Well," he said quietly, while Willie Hardy stooped and quietly picked up the pieces of silver and transferred them to his pocket, "we players are about to have a secret session; none but the members of the eleven may attend. Now, as you are no longer a player, you must get out."

"But you have no authority to put me off the team."

"I have; I have had permission for the last month from Mr. Keenan to put you out just as soon as I find you unbearable."

"You're a liar!" cried Snowden, white with rage.

Claude had not been practicing self-denial on and off the field in vain. He bit his lips.

"Well, since you won't go out, I shall have to call Mr. Keenan."

"You won't do anything of the sort, you wretched little tattle-tale!" bawled Snowden, planting himself in front of the open door. "If you try to get out—"

He has not finished that sentence to the present day. For Claude, with a spring and a twist, seized Snowden's neck in a mighty grasp, turned him round, jerked him sprawling into the corridor without and, before anyone realized what had happened, shut the door and locked it.

When he turned around again, he was smiling.

"I think I did the right thing, boys."

"I don't know about that," said Pierson. "Since you can handle him so easily, you might as well have given him a kick as a souvenir. If I had your strength, I'd have done it."

"There he goes," said O'Rourke, who was gazing out of the window; "and he looks as if he had had enough of Claude Lightfoot."

"You made a mistake at the very beginning of the season in being so easy with him, Claude," said Archer. "He thought you were afraid of him."

"So I was; I was afraid of losing him. Perhaps if I had been stiffer, he would have come to time. But it's over now, thank God."

"Perhapth," lisped Willie, "Erneth Thnowden will give away our thignals to the other thide."

"That's the way you talk about your friends,

is it?" said Desmond. "Those of us here who dislike him most would never imagine such a thing of him."

"Well, to business, boys," said Claude. "I think that now we have a better team than ever. I'll play halfback in place of Snowden, and Harry Archer may play in his old position at quarter. It's better all around."

"Remember, Claude, I am not in good condition; and besides, I don't know the signals as well as the rest. I have to think them out."

"So much the better in one way. If I were playing quarter, I might give them out too fast. But you will have to think before you call the numbers, and so every player will have time to know exactly what he's expected to do."

Then the eleven went into a discussion of various plays and their details. They concluded their conference in high spirits, and as they dispersed, Dockery observed:

"If it were not for Hardy I should be willing to bet dollars to cents that we should win."

Chapter XII

IN WHICH MR. KEENAN FACES AN INDIGNANT MOTHER AND IS MORE FRIGHTENED THAN HE EVER WAS SINCE HE CAME TO THE USE OF REASON

"MR. Keenan, there's a lady in the parlor to see you," said the porter of Milwaukee College, as, in response to his bell, the prefect descended the stairs.

Mr. Keenan passed his hand through his hair.

"I dare say it's some new trouble," he muttered, for he had just received the news of Snowden's expulsion from the team.

On entering the parlor, a woman who had been seated very erect, and with lips compressed, arose and faced him.

"Mr. Keenan?"

"Yes, madam."

"I am Mrs. Snowden, and I have just called here to tell you what I think of your college athletics."

"Sit down, Mrs. Snowden," and Mr. Keenan drew up a chair and, after her, seated himself.

"College athletics have been the ruin of my boy."

"Indeed! I am sorry to hear it."

"Perhaps, you have reason to be sorry, Mr. Keenan; for I understand that you have made great efforts to foster athletics in this college."

Mr. Keenan bowed his head. He had nothing to say yet; for he was wise enough to see that Mrs. Snowden would not be prepared to hear the other side until she had expressed her sentiments at length.

"For the last two years," continued the mother, "I have noticed that my boy has been steadily going down in his studies. In First Academic, he was one of the leaders in his class studies; in Humanities, he joined the football team and got only an average place in the class; in Poetry, it was, if anything, worse; and now that he's in Rhetoric, I find from his bulletin for September and October that he has failed in three branches of the bi-monthly competitions, Latin, Greek and Mathematics."

"That is too bad," murmured Mr. Keenan sympathetically. He did not think the time had yet come for him to speak.

"Indeed it is. But there are the athletics. Just as soon as he started to play football in the college eleven, he gave up study. Whereas before he used to stay home every night and give two or more hours to study,

he began in Humanities to talk football and
go out to see his friends and *fellow athletes.*"
The last part of this sentence was touched
heavily with scorn.

"Did you encourage Ernest to go out, Mrs.
Snowden?"

"Indeed, I did not. It is true, he began
dancing lessons in Humanities; but that took
only one night in the week. And then, of
course, I had no objection to his going to a
party now and then; but rarely, mind you."

"And, perhaps, you allowed him to go occasionally to the theater?"

"On that point I have been very strict. I
never allow Ernest to go more than twice
in the month. But we are getting away from
the point. This year, despite my convictions,
I allowed Ernest to go into the college eleven.
He begged me so hard that I couldn't bring
myself to refuse him. So he joins the eleven,
contributes money and sacrifices his Thursday recreations in coming here to practice;
and, as I expected, neglects his studies on
account of athletics. And now after the sacrifice of time and studies, he is coolly
informed an hour ago by that impudent captain of yours that he cannot play in the
great Thanksgiving-Day game this afternoon.
And now he is disgraced. He was announced

in the papers several times as one of Milwaukee College's best players. All his friends and the family's friends are looking to see what he will do; and when he does not appear in the game, they will find that he has been put off the team. It is bad enough that he should lose his reputation as a student, but this makes it worse a thousand times. I think my boy has a right to play on your team, and I demand it."

Mrs. Snowden, as she made this statement of Ernest's wrongs, had been on the point of going into tears, but mastered herself and stood upon her rights. Had she followed her womanly impulse, she would have won the day, and Mr. Keenan would have missed the chance of conveying some of his favorite views on the subject of athletics and studies. But her imperative demand nerved him to do what he considered his duty.

"Excuse me, Mrs. Snowden, if I appear to contradict you, but I fear your boy has no right to play on the team."

Mrs. Snowden drew herself up and gazed steadily at the timid prefect. She could have done nothing better to take away his timidity.

"And more, he shall not play on the team, at least for this season. And if I am here next season he shall not play then, unless he brings a note from you to the effect that you desire him to play and that you will answer for his going into proper training. I say, he shall not play this season. The first thing that we require of a football player is obedience to the captain. Ernest has been disobedient to the point of contumacy. Today he acted in such a manner toward Claude Lightfoot, who is as gentlemanly and long-suffering a captain as one could wish to have, that if Claude had not put your boy out of the team, I fear I should have had to do so myself. The second point, also of great importance in a team, is discipline and training. Of all the eleven, Ernest has been the least satisfactory. Why even last night, I have just been informed, he was at a party which broke up at twelve o'clock."

"But he told me that the players were expected to relax themselves before the game."

"Not in that kind of a way," answered Mr. Keenan grimly. He felt that he was facing a "foolish" mother, and he was determined to let her hear the truth whatever pain it might cost him or her. Surgical operations are sometimes necessary.

"And now," he proceeded, "I wish to turn back to the original point. You implied that

I had helped to the ruin of your boy as a student by encouraging him in athletics. You also attached the blame of his failures in classwork to football. You remarked that from the class of Humanities to Rhetoric, he has been going down steadily; and you insisted that this period of football has also been his period of deterioration. Have I put your case clearly, madam?"

"Yes, sir," answered Mrs. Snowden, beginning to grow timid and nervous. Mr. Keenan was too excited to observe the change in her manner; had he noticed it, he would have been frightened.

"You also remarked that in the class of Humanities, he began to go to dancing school."

"I did, sir; surely you have no objection to that?"

"If you please, I had rather not enter into that question," answered the wily prefect. He preferred to pass over a point concerning which "there was a great deal to be said on both sides" and gain a coign of vantage where he was surer of his position.

"So, then," he continued, "Ernest's deterioration in study coincides exactly with his dancing lessons as well as with his football practice."

"Pardon me, Mr. Keenan!" cried Mrs. Snowden, now entirely on the defensive, "but he stopped dancing lessons last year in January after attending for only fourteen months, whereas he has been at football for three years."

"Which means exactly seven months for football as against fourteen months for dancing. But you also remarked yourself that from the time he began to play football, he began to go out at night a great deal."

"Yes; and I repeat it emphatically."

"Might you not have said as well that from the time he began to go to dancing school he began to go out at night time?"

"I—I—no—I think not," gasped Mrs. Snowden weakly.

"And might you not as well have said," pursued Mr. Keenan relentlessly, "that from the time he began to go out at night time, he began to neglect his studies?"

Mrs. Snowden was dazed. No answer came from her lips.

"And again, you say that from the time he took to athletics, he began to neglect his studies. Doubtless you are in good faith about that. But so far is this from being the case that the very opposite is true."

Mrs. Snowden looked very much astonished, as indeed she was.

"Here is the exact truth. From the time that Ernest began to neglect athletics he began to neglect his studies."

"I beg your pardon, Mr. Keenan?"

"I have had occasion to look up the history of your boy at this college, and what I have just stated is, I am convinced, true. Why was it that Ernest was selected when in Humanities to play in the college football eleven? It was because in the preceding year he was the best all-round athlete among the younger students. During his three years in the three Academic classes, I find that he gave much attention to baseball and football, to running, to jumping and to gymnasium work. Instead of going to the theater or to dancing school, or to seeing his athletic friends—we shall return to that point presently—he spent his evenings at home and gave two or three hours to his studies. Then he went to bed before ten o'clock and got up a little before seven."

"How did you learn all that?" cried Mrs. Snowden.

"I had special reasons for inquiring into the matter," answered the prefect; "and now I am very glad that I did so. Accordingly, during his fourteenth year, and his fifteenth, and his sixteenth, Ernest was leading what I consider a student's ideal life. He developed mind and body, and when he entered the class of Humanities, he was so well trained physically and mentally that he was unanimously chosen as a member of the college football team. Now it is an actual fact that from that time to the present he has fallen in studies and done little more than hold his place in athletics. Had he continued to live the same life during Humanities, Poetry and Rhetoric as he had led in the three Academic classes, I dare say that he would be the leading boy in the college whether on the field or in the classroom. Instead of that, he has remained almost stationary in athletics and he has retrograded in studies."

"I think," said Mrs. Snowden, making as if to rise, "that I have taken enough of your time."

"I can spare a few minutes yet, madam. Now why did Ernest decline in studies? You put it upon athletics. I see no reason for agreeing with you. Athletics and studies go well together. There is, so far as I can learn, no opposition between them. The 'sound mind in the sound body' is a saying sanctioned by the ages. When a boy, I attended boarding school and played in every baseball and football game that I could. I was healthy and strong and never found that these sports interfered with my lessons, except now and then. Looking back, I find that when they did interfere, it was owing to the fact that I had played too much. But this is no argument against athletics. In all things, study or work or exercise, excess is wrong. We must distinguish between the use of a thing and the abuse. I remember that in my time at St. Maure's, and I attended that College for five years, the very best athletes, some thirty or more in all, were with but two exceptions, high up in their classes. Of these two exceptions, one, I know, was what they call a ladies' man; the other's ill-success in studies I could not account for."

"Do you mean to say," said Mrs. Snowden, "that success in athletics means success in studies?"

"Not at all, Mrs. Snowden; but I do mean to say that success in athletics so far from being a bar to success in studies is rather a help. The two run together nicely. On the other hand, it has been my experience that studies and social amusements—balls, parties, dancing schools—do not go together at all."

Mrs. Snowden thought she perceived an opening.

"So, then," she cried, raising her head, "you would take my boy from the society of his more refined friends, the young ladies and young gentlemen, and keep him in the company of the rude football player. I must say, Mr. Keenan, that I cannot quite agree with you."

"I did not expect you to agree with me, Mrs. Snowden," answered the prefect somewhat brusquely. "Because if you did agree with me, you would not have acted as you have."

"Perhaps," said Mrs. Snowden sarcastically, "you would favor the system of the Medes for training boys; put them together and let them grow up disciplined barbarians."

"No, I should not favor that system at all. The boy who has the refining influence of sisters and parents at home, provided he is shielded from bad or silly companions, lives under the best system we can hope to enjoy."

"But that is not enough, Mr. Keenan. I don't want my boy to be a boor after finishing college."

"That is impossible, madam, with the home influence which he has. But it is a mistake to think that fine bowing is better than strong thinking, that the gift of entering a parlor gracefully is of more importance than the gift of handling an idea gracefully. Putting aside such questions, you assume what I cannot grant, namely, that the boy whose sentiments are unhealthily developed through his aping, in common with other young people, the ways of grown men and women in society has better manners than other boys who lead the simple, healthy, studious lives which I firmly believe God intended them to live. What little experience I have leads me to a different conclusion. That boy has the best manners who has the best home; and that boy has the best home who has a prudent mother, a wise father, and good sisters, and manly, honest brothers."

Mrs. Snowden was not convinced; but she was silenced.

"Another point, Mrs. Snowden," continued Mr. Keenan in answer to her silence. "You spoke of Ernest's going out at nights to visit his athletic friends. Pardon me if I ask: were his athletic friends mostly boys?"

Mrs. Snowden, by way of answer to the question, took out her handkerchief and began to sob.

"Oh, I beg your pardon! I have been rude!" cried Mr. Keenan, turning pale with fright, jumping to his feet and bringing his hands together. "Please don't cry! I really can't stand it. I am very sorry! I—I'll try to make it all right, Mrs. Snowden. If you send your boy to me after dinner, I'll have a talk with him and try to arrange matters. And I'll see Claude Lightfoot, too, and do my best to bring about an understanding. I'm really very sorry for hurting your feelings. In my excitement, I quite forgot myself."

There were drops of perspiration on the prefect's face.

Mrs. Snowden wiped her eyes and rose.

"Don't apologize, Mr. Keenan; I—I—was thinking about my poor boy. Perhaps I have made mistakes, but I meant to act for the best, and—and—I love him."

"And I love him!" How I wish that every one of us who have to deal with troublesome boys could constantly keep before us this little text of four words. The ugly, sullen, willful, disobedient boy may be very insignificant in our eyes. But there is his mother, there is his father, there are his sisters. They see with better, purer eyes than ours, and they love him. While we may be thinking of crushing him, fond prayers from tender hearts may be storming the gates of Heaven for that poor creature's sake. Innocent cheeks, cheeks worn with suffering, may be wet with tears that are shed for love of him. He may be black and forbidding as he appears in the range of our limited vision, but the mother who caught with ecstasy his first sweet infant smile, who heard with swelling heart his first fond words of endearment, who watched every beautiful trait of his budding character—the mother, I say, sees with other, larger eyes than ours; with eyes, God be thanked for it, that are nearest in their vision to the eyes of Him who is to be judge of that boy and of those who, for a brief moment his judges, are to face the same tribunal. "And I love him!" Above the mist and the cloud, behind the veil, there is One Other who utters with even more tenderness the mother's touching cry.

Mrs. Snowden was fond and foolish. But who shall condemn her for her foolishness? Living in surroundings where "society" notions—worldly notions, to put it more clearly—were in the air, she had acted according to the prejudices which, alas, are too common today, which are turning out namby-pambies of both sexes year after year, which are overthrowing sound mental training and promising to foist upon the coming century pale young women who were in society when they should have been in pinafores, and effeminate young men who were trying to fancy themselves in love when they should have been schooling themselves for the hard and inevitable struggle of life.

Chapter XIII

ON THE WAY TO THE FOOTBALL FIELD

THREE omnibuses were standing in line in front of the college building on State Street. The first one contained the football eleven, Mr. Keenan, Father Hogan, who was a lover of athletics, and Ed Coale, a small boy dressed in a football suit, who was supposed to be the club's mascot. In the other two were some forty or fifty students, splendid with flags, with horns and with streamers of gold, white and blue, the college colors. They were uproariously noisy; and what with the blowing of horns, the yelling of college cries and the pushing and crowding for positions, the picture was one that would make an old man feel young again.

In the players' 'bus there was no crowding and, in consequence, less confusion.

"Everybody here?" cried Mr. Keenan.

"Where's Archer?" asked Claude, looking around.

"He was looking for a pair of scapulars just a minute ago," Gerald O'Rourke made answer. "Ah, here he comes now! Did you get them?" he continued, as Harry leaped lightly over the steps into the 'bus.

"Yes; I was determined to get them. I'd as soon think of going swimming without my scapulars on as play a game of football without them."

"Swimming is far more dangerous, though," said Claude.

"You ought to wear your thcapulars all the time," said Willie Hardy.

"So I do; but somehow or other I mislaid my pair this morning and came away without them."

Everybody having settled into his place, Mr. Keenan gave the driver the order to start.

"Just one yell before we go!" cried O'Neil. "All ready, boys!"

Then seventy vigorous throats filled the air with—

Hoopla—hoopla—hoopla—who?
'Rah for the gold and white and blue!

As the first 'bus started, the small boys, not to be ignored, shouted their yell, an importation from Georgetown College. They gave nearly every mystic word a jerk, and the effect was not unlike the multitudinous explosions of firecrackers under a barrel.

Hiki—hiki—hai—kai
Muki mori—hai—yai!
To my mori
To my dori
Muki mori—hai—yai!

"Hold on a moment!" shouted Harry Archer to the driver. "Here comes Father Trainer, boys. Come this way, Father. Jump right in."

Father Trainer, who had been awakened by the unusual disturbance from the intricacies of a mathematical formula to the remembrance of the great football game, had at once hurried down to catch the 'bus. His collar and tie were somewhat twisted, giving him the appearance of a man who had been recently throttled. He seated himself next to Harry, who arranged his beloved coach's neck-gear.

"I'm glad you've come, Father."

"I'm glad myself; when I heard that you were going to play, I made up my mind to come; and I'm sure that if you are as quick in football as in geometry, you will win the game all by yourself."

Harry laughed.

"It takes eleven to win a game, Father. As for myself"— here Harry became grave —"I'm not in very good condition, and I feel as if something were going to happen to me."

"Don't let that feeling stay; kick it out," said Claude. "You are all right; you look first-rate. And just look around at the team that is going to back you up—aren't they a fine-looking set? Since going into training they have nearly all gained weight. The average weight of our team is now one hundred and forty-nine."

"They all look somewhat pale," observed Father Trainer, "except that rather pretty boy with the smiling face and innocent expression."

"The pale fellows, Father," said Claude, "have the pallor of health; men in good training are not very red-cheeked. As for that pretty boy, his red cheeks fool everybody. He is the only boy on the eleven not in good condition."

"Yes, and his innocent expression and sweet smile fool people, too," said Dockery. "But," he added, noticing the expression on Claude's face, "I shouldn't have said that. It was uncharitable, and I went to Communion this morning."

"I wish I had gone," sighed Harry. "But I had no idea I was to play."

"All of us poets in the eleven went," said O'Rourke. "And I prayed, first that we might win, secondly that no one might get hurt."

"I put it just the other way," said Claude.

"It would have been better," observed the prefect, "if you had prayed first to play a gentlemanly but hard game, and then put in the other two points in Claude's order."

"Don't look so glum, Harry," whispered Father Trainer. "Why today surely you should have nothing on your mind. You graduated in geometry last night; and remember what I told you—don't look at a book on mathematics till after the contest. You are splendidly prepared, and a few days' rest will put your brains in the best possible condition. And as you need rest I am glad you are playing football. The most perfect rest for a student is that manner of pleasurable occupation which will most completely take away his mind from his studies. Football takes away the student player's mind most completely. Q. E. D."

"Yes, Father; but remember that to play football, a boy ought to be in training; otherwise he is far more likely to get hurt. Now, suppose I should be laid up and couldn't make that examination."

"I'll not suppose any such thing!" exclaimed Father Trainer vehemently. "Don't you let your imagination scare you, Harry."

"Then, there's another thing that's troubling me, Father."

"Something else, Harry?"

"Yes; today will be my last game with the boys. You know, Father, because I've told you, how poor we are at home. Well, ways and means are getting worse every day. There is now no reasonable hope of our paying the interest on the mortgage due toward the middle of December. Several new bills have cropped up that we knew nothing about, and we haven't ten dollars in the world today. Then you remember how I told you about those shares we own in a silver mine?"

"Perfectly, Harry. If I am not mistaken, it was on the hope of their being of some value that your mother insisted on your continuing to go to school."

"Well, Father, we got word lately from the

man who is running the mine that there is no present hope of its being a paying concern. So that takes the last prop from under us. On hearing the news, I almost insisted on going to work; and my mother yielded somewhat reluctantly. Last vacation I was working at a hardware store for six dollars a week. The same position is now open to me at seven and one-half; and I am wanted as soon as possible. So I start in tomorrow morning."

"But what about your mathematical contest?" cried Father Trainer.

"Oh, I've arranged for that; I'm to be free that day. But, do you know, Father, I am a little nervous. I never felt that way before, and I've played every season. What is more, I never was hurt in a game. But today I feel that I am not just right. Nothing would have got me into playing, if I had not thought that I was really needed."

"Say a *Hail Mary* before each half," suggested Gerald O'Rourke. "I've always done that before every half, and I've never had a scratch."

"When I wath at Thaint Maureth," volunteered Willie Hardy, "the boyth of the eleven uthed to go to the chapel in a body and thay the beadth and the litany on their kneeth."

"Well, why don't you keep up their record?" inquired Collins brusquely. "The whole crowd of us went to the chapel before we came out, but we didn't see you on your knees. You stood out in the corridor while we were praying, to tell John, the janitor—whose eyes, as he rested on his broom, were sticking out of his head—one of your thrilling adventures with Indians at St. Maure's. You nearly spoiled my prayer where you told how you knocked an Indian senseless with one blow of your strong right hand while throttling his fierce hunting-dog with your left."

"It wath a joke," said Willie.

Chapter XIV

IN WHICH MANDOLIN MERRY AND MARY DALE LEARN SOMETHING OF THE GREAT GAME

THE football game between the Central High School eleven, made up of Milwaukee's chosen high-school students, and the Milwaukee College team was to begin at three o'clock sharp. At a quarter-past two there were already some three hundred people on the grounds—mostly boys. These young gentlemen, very lively as to their movements, very gay with colors—crimson for the Centrals, and white and gold and blue for the Milwaukees—were crowding about the ropes, which were so arranged as to give the players plenty of room.

Within the ropes was the "gridiron," so called from the appearance which it presents to the spectator. The gridiron is described by an expert as "a rectangular field three hundred and thirty feet long, and one hundred and sixty feet wide. This space is enclosed by heavy white lines marked upon the ground. From one end to the other are also marked in lime twenty-one lines, each one distant five yards from the next. Of these lines, the fifth is marked much more heavily than the others and is known as the 'twenty-five-yard line.'" Among the spectators in the "grandstand" of the park, three young ladies and two small boys were seated, gazing at the gridiron with no little perplexity.

Frankie Elmwood Lightfoot was the smaller boy. He looked very like Claude and was wriggling with impatience. Beside him was Paul Archer. Two of the young ladies we have seen before; the smaller, a girl of fourteen, was Miss Mandolin Merry, who, as the reader may remember, had extorted a promise from Willie Hardy not to injure Claude Lightfoot. Miss Mandolin Merry was one of Alice's pupils and was sitting just now beside the grave professor of music. Mandolin knew as much of football as she did of the principles of poetry, a study in which she was supposed to be then engaged. She made a distinction, however, between the game and the players, and had come to watch the latter, especially the heroic Willie Hardy. The third young lady was Mary Dale, a fellow graduate and dear friend of Alice's.

"What is that place marked out in white?" asked Frank Lightfoot.

"I think they call it the frying pan," volunteered Mandolin, who was chewing Adams' tutti-frutti.

Alice giggled.

"Gridiron, you mean. But what are all those lines running across for?"

"I wish some of the boys would come and talk to us," continued Mandolin. "It's dull sitting here with no one to talk to."

Alice and Mary smiled at the ingenuous remark of Mandolin.

Suddenly Frankie Lightfoot darted from

his place, made a plunge forward and disappeared over the next seat as though he had made a dive, his left foot coming in contact with the broad shoulders of a man who was sitting in front of our party. The man turned savagely, but on perceiving the pair of tiny legs that were describing all kinds of motions, he seized the one that came handiest and brought young Frankie into evidence again. The urchin was scarcely on his feet when he rushed down as far as the grandstand permitted and bawled at the top of his voice:

"Frank Elmwood! Hi! Hi! O Frank!"

The person whom he thus invoked had just entered the gate and was walking toward the ropes. He gave no sign of hearing these adjurations.

"Lend me that horn!" cried Frank excitedly to a small boy sitting in the lowest row.

Frank grasped it feverishly and gave three loud blasts, then bawled:

"Hey, Frank! Frank Elmwood! Godfather!"

He was plaintive in his yelling, and really pathetic on the word "Godfather."

The crowd in the grandstand laughed and applauded.

"Come here, Godfather!" continued Frankie.

"Hey, Godfather, Godfather!" yelled at least

a dozen boys. Then nearly every Junior student of Milwaukee College joined in till the field rang with their invocation.

"Come here, Godfather!"

Even the small boys hugging the ropes turned toward the grandstand.

Then the scattering of boys who had called for Godfather took out their horns and blew them bravely. Frank Elmwood, in common with every person on the field, turned grinningly toward the center of disturbance. Little Lightfoot thereupon leaped upon the railing and, supporting himself by holding to an upright with one hand, gesticulated violently with the other. Alice and Mary gave a little shriek and hastened down to rescue the brother of Claude.

That young gentleman, utterly unconscious of his own danger and of the gaze of four hundred people, was absorbed in catching Elmwood's eye. Naturally he caught it.

"Come here, Frank! Come here, my God—"

It sounded very like profanity, but Alice jerked the youngster from his perch in the middle of the word, and so it stands misleading and unfinished.

Elmwood now discovered that all these lively demonstrations had reference to him. Blushing violently, he made toward the grandstand while the malicious Milwaukee students, who happened to know Elmwood's spiritual relationship with the little man struggling and kicking in Alice's arms, filled the air with tooting of horns and high-pitched adjurations to the Godfather.

"Say, Frank!" cried the youngster, jumping up into the young correspondent's arms and jumping down again, "say, I want you to sit by me and tell me about the game. This boy is Paul Archer; he's a good fellow and not a bit stingy. Whenever he has candy, he gives me lots. This girl is Alice Archer; she's a nice girl, and this girl," continued Frankie, hardly giving Elmwood time to bow and utter the briefest conventionalities, "is Mary Dale; she's the right sort of a girl too. That there one," concluded Frankie with a jerk of his thumb toward Mandolin, "is Mandolin Merry; she's n.g."

"Frankie!" cried Alice.

"Oh, you needn't look! She's mean to me and Paul. We were with her in the same car all the way to the game, and she didn't take any notice of us. I didn't mind that so much, neither did Paul. But she didn't give us any candy and ate a whole boxful herself. She is mean; we don't like her, and she don't like us."

"Why," said Elmwood to Mandolin, whose

complexion had grown suddenly rich, "I've heard of you often, and was informed that you were very fond of boys."

"Not that size of boy!" said Mandolin tartly.

Frank, Alice and Mary looked at each other for one moment. Then Mary pulled out her handkerchief and buried her face in it; Alice coughed violently, while the correspondent struggled manfully with his risible muscles. Mandolin meanwhile glared at the *enfant terrible* and wondered whether she had said anything ridiculous. Her sense of humor was somewhat inferior to Willie Hardy's.

"I am very glad to meet you, Miss Archer," said Elmwood, recovering himself. "I've had the pleasure of seeing your brother Harry on the football field and have conceived the greatest admiration for him. He plays with character."

"I don't quite understand," said Alice.

"Well, he puts his whole energy into the game, never relaxes, never gives up, and always goes in for fair play. I think that a boy who plays in that fashion has character, for such a style of play means courage, endurance, perseverance and self-control."

"Thank you, Mr. Elmwood. I like to hear people praise my brother because I think he's the nicest boy in Milwaukee almost, except perhaps your brother, Mary, and Claude Lightfoot, Frankie, and your brother Tom, Mandolin."

Mandolin looked pleased. She really loved her brother and liked to hear him praised. And, to do him justice, Tom was a very good fellow, indeed.

"The best piece of news I have heard in a long time," continued Frank Elmwood, "is that Harry Archer is to play, after all. He's the best quarterback in the city."

"And isn't Claude good, Frank?" said the small boy.

"Yes, indeed. For all-around playing, he has no superior, I believe. Possibly several of the other side are his equal, but I doubt it. Claude has grown very strong the last year. Besides, there is originality in his play. He brings in his running and jumping and strength where most other boys would not know how to use them."

"Do you think the Milwaukee College boys will win?" asked Mary.

"Well, I'm a little afraid. Of the eleven players, nine are first-rate. They are in splendid training; they know their signals as well as one could wish, and most of them are absolutely fearless. But then, one of the players is in poor condition. He is a cigarette fiend and, I am told, has been running around at night. The worst of it is that the Centrals know of him and, in all probability, will direct their plays against him. I'm beginning to fear that he will lose the game for our boys."

"Haven't they anyone to put in his place?" asked Alice.

"Yes; George Hastings. But although he is very quick and a good tackler and quite fearless, he is much too young and too light. In case of necessity he will have to come into the game, but even then I am of opinion that the tackle opposing him will make an opening every time for the runner with the ball."

"Willie Hardy," put in Mandolin, who had recovered her self-possession and a simper, "told me that things were not at all as bright even as you make them, Mr. Elmwood. He said that hardly any of the eleven were in condition to play."

"Is that so?" said Frank with a twinkle. "I'm afraid Willie is exaggerating. The fact is that the only boy in the team not in training is Willie himself."

"Isn't he one of the touchdowns?" asked Mandolin.

"Not exactly."

"Then he's a ghoul, isn't he?"

"He may be a ghoul for all I know. But in

the college eleven he plays left tackle."

"Say, Frank, explain the game to us, won't you?" put in Paul. "Why do they call it football?"

"Because once on a time they used to use their feet in it mostly. But nowadays it is all changed. In most cases the ball is carried. Almost the only time that the ball is kicked is when they can't do anything else with it."

"How do they decide who wins the game?" inquired Alice.

"They decide by the points made. You see that gridiron there? Well, the object each side has in view is to bring the ball down into the opponents' territory and carry it across the goal line. Every time a side does that it scores four points. You see all those lines running from side to side? They mark each five yards. The furthest line of all at each end is the goal line. If the opposing side gets the ball past that, there is a score of four points. Then the side that has scored has the privilege of taking the ball out as far as is judged convenient and proper—and one of the players, trained for that purpose, must try to kick it over and between those goalposts. If they kick it over, they score two points more, and then the game begins over again from the middle of the field. The game is divided into two halves, each of thirty-five minutes. At the end of the second half, the side which has made the most points is decided winner."

"But how do they begin?" asked Mary, who had never attended a game before.

"They begin by what is called a kick-off. The two captains ordinarily throw up a coin for choice, and the captain who wins may choose either the goal which he prefers, or leave the choice of goal to the other captain and instead take the privilege of kicking off the ball. Suppose he chooses the kick-off. Then the other side takes whichever goal they please. If the wind is high, it is an advantage to choose the goal which is to leeward. Well, the side that has the kick-off gets in a line just behind or nearly even with the ball which is placed in precisely the center of the field, which is on the middle point of the eleventh five-yard line. The other side ranges themselves in different parts of the field, each one at least ten yards back of the center line, and wait for the kick-off. Then when the ball is kicked, the opponent who can catch it does so, while the others of his side gather around him to guard him. He then tries to run forward towards the other side's goal as far as he can. Of course, the side that has the kick-off runs after the ball and tries to down the

fellow who catches it before he can bring it
back. As soon as they down him—"

"What do you mean by downing him?"
Mary interrupted.

"Tackling him successfully, that is, catching hold of him in such a manner that he
cannot advance further. Generally when a
man is tackled he comes to the ground and
is down. Well, after the runner with the ball
is so downed, the referee, who judges the
amount of space gained by the runner,
announces, 'First down, five yards to gain.'
and then we have a scrimmage."

"Who plays the scrimmage?" This question
came from Mandolin.

"Everybody plays in the scrimmage. The
side that has the ball lines up. They must
stand in such a way that they are not in
front of the ball. The forwards or rushers are
standing pretty close together. The center rush
holds the ball and, at a signal, passes it back
to the man behind him who is called the
quarterback. This man cannot run forward
with the ball, but must pass it to some third
man behind him. The third man will then try
to go forward with the ball while the other
side, who have lined up to stop this forward
movement, try to break through their opponents' line or to go round the ends and tackle

the runner. Suppose they succeed in holding
him after he has advanced one yard beyond
the spot where the ball was originally placed;
then he has made one out of the five yards,
and the referee announces 'Second down, four
yards to gain.' Then they have another scrimmage in just the same way. Suppose that
this time the man who has been called out
to run with the ball does not succeed in
making any gain; in that case the referee
calls, 'Third down, four yards to gain.' Now
if they fail to make their four yards in this
third scrimmage, they lose the ball."

"So," put in Alice, "the side that has the
ball after the kick-off is obliged to make five
yards in three trials, or hand over the ball
to the opponents?"

"Yes, unless they lose twenty yards instead
of gaining five. In that case, they keep the
ball."

"But how could they lose twenty yards?"
asked Mary.

"Why, they might be forced backwards, or
the runner might run toward his own goal
either on purpose or in order to get away
from a tackler."

"Oh, I see. So then they keep on playing
up and down the field till one side or the
other manages to get the ball over the oppo-

nents' goal line."

"That is the ordinary way of playing, Miss Dale. Sometimes, however, instead of carrying the ball, it is kicked. For instance, the side with the ball has made only one yard of the five in two trials, or has even lost ground. The captain thinks that his side will not be able to make the five yards in the third trial, and, as he is going to lose the ball anyhow, he resolves to lose it as near the opponents' goal as possible. He gives the signal, the center snaps the ball back to the quarter who throws it to one of the halfbacks or to the fullback. The man who gets it, instead of rushing forward with it, kicks it as far as he can down the field. The chances now are that the other side will secure the ball, but even so it will be twenty-five or thirty yards further down than it would otherwise have been."

Just at this moment a great shout arose from the small boys, which was at once taken up by the crowd till it swelled into a roar, diversified by the braying of horns and the blare of a few trumpets. The people seated in the grandstand and on the "bleachers" arose, and canes gaudy with colors, handkerchiefs swayed by jewelled hands, waving banners of gold and white and blue, or of crimson, made the scene a veritable pleasure to the eye. The cause of this demonstration was the entrance of the Milwaukees onto the field. They came running in lightly, though, despite the ease of their movements, they could not but look awkward and ungainly in their tight-laced canvas jackets and their stuffed canvas knee-breeches. The football suit is of a piece with the style of playing; elegance and grace are sacrificed to effectiveness.

"Why," exclaimed a man near our group, "those fellows won't stand any chance against the Centrals! They are much too light. There's one there who is a small boy; he can't weigh over one hundred pounds. I wonder: does he intend to play?"

"Not unless someone is hurt," volunteered Elmwood. "That boy is George Hastings. He is as good a tackler as I've seen but is far too young and too light."

"Don't you think the whole team is too light?" Alice asked of Frank.

"Well, yes. They have brought themselves up to average one hundred and forty-nine; but the Centrals average one hundred and fifty-eight, a difference in their favor of about one hundred pounds."

Again a great roar arose from the spectators, and this time the bright dresses of young ladies and the crimson colors were very much in evidence as the Centrals, victors in five contests, and not once defeated in the present season, came marching onto the field. It was their proud boast that no team thus far had even scored against them; and to the confidence which comes of success, they added the caution and care which good coaching is wont to foster. They intended to win the game; in their minds, there was no question about that. But they also were bent upon doing everything in their power to prevent the Milwaukees from scoring a touchdown. They well knew that it was a difficult matter to tackle Claude Lightfoot if he should once get into the open field guarded by Harry Archer; they recognized Dockery's skill in hitting the line; but, on the other hand, they had learned that Snowden was not to play—Snowden who could hit the center for a gain of from three to nine yards, where others would be downed on the line; and, best of all, they counted, when playing on the defensive, on breaking through Hardy and tackling the Milwaukee runner before he could get fairly started.

The Milwaukee team were by no means so sanguine about their prospect. They felt fairly certain that they should be able to score with Lightfoot, Dockery and, above all, Archer; they were sure that, even should they find the opposing line too strong, they would get in some magnificent run down the field on one or the other of the "trick" plays which these players knew how to employ. But the absence of Snowden was a decided loss; and the presence of Willie Hardy, out of condition as he was, promised disaster. Moreover, should any player be disabled, it would be necessary to call in George Hastings; and the team in that case, light as it now was, would be too weakened to stand the hard rushes of the Central's heavy backs. In a word, their hope of winning the game was very faint.

"Claude!" called Mr. Keenan, who, surrounded by a crowd of Milwaukee students, was standing at the ropes near the northern goal.

"Well, sir!" cried Claude, smiling and touching his cap, as he ran over to the prefect.

"I promised Mrs. Snowden this morning to let her boy play, if I could bring it about. Of course, he should be obliged to apologize to you and the eleven for his conduct. I saw him a little while ago, but he would not agree. It's too bad."

"We might let him play anyhow, sir, in case someone is disabled."

"No," said Mr. Keenan decidedly. "I think we have gone far enough to let him play under any conditions. I am sorry; but we must make the best of it."

While the crowd was shouting, laughing at and applauding the practice work of the two elevens, which, of course, was of the lightest nature, the two captains came together and, after discussing a few points, tossed up for choice of goal or kick-off. Seawell, the captain of the Central High School eleven, won the toss and, as there was little or no wind blowing, without hesitation chose the ball. Claude took the northern goal.

A moment later the teams fell into position for the "kick-off." The Centrals, who had possession of the ball, ranged themselves on a line extending the breadth of the gridiron just a little behind the center line, so as to take a flying start with the ball as it was kicked down the field. The Milwaukees, on the other hand, selected various positions ranging from fifteen to forty yards from the kick-off line, in such wise that no point where the ball might be kicked was left unguarded. As the ball was placed on the center of the fifty-five yard line, a sudden silence came over the spectators, now numbering some twelve hundred. The excitement was tense. Then the fullback of the Centrals, who had gone some fifteen yards behind the ball, came

on at an easy run and, as his fellow players stepped forward for their start, kicked
the ball high and straight down the field.

The greatest game of the year had begun.

Chapter XV

*IN WHICH THE MILWAUKEES PLAY THE FIRST HALF
UNDER DIFFICULTIES*

BEFORE going on with the game, it may
be well, for the sake of the enthusiast
in football, to furnish the names and positions of the opposing elevens. The "line-up"
was as follows:

Milwaukee College		Central High School
Walter Collins	Left End	Tracy Lupper
Willie Hardy	Left Tackle	Henry Hartman
Francis Stein	Left Guard	Charles Lamb
Charles Pierson	Center	Edward King
John Drew	Right Guard	Howard Stockton
Gerald O'Rourke	Right Tackle	George Fox
Andrew O'Neil	Right End	Willis Andrews
Harry Archer	Quarterback	Roy Becker
Dan Dockery	Left Halfback	Ray Monroe
Claude Lightfoot (Capt.)	Right Halfback	George Walker
Maurice Desmond	Fullback	Charles Seawell (Capt.)

The game, the greatest game of the year, I repeat, had begun, when Seawell, captain of the Centrals, sent the ball spinning into the air and straight toward his opponent's goal.

It was a long kick, and the wearers of the crimson lining the ropes and seated in the bleachers broke into a yell of delight.

"Lightfoot! Lightfoot!" cried the sympathizers with the Milwaukee College.

Claude was standing on the ten-yard line directly in front of the goal, and the ball was coming straight toward him. It was a splendid kick, the Milwaukee College people admitted, but it was going straight to the right man in the right place; and while the Milwaukees rushed toward Claude to guard him after his catch, and the Centrals dashed down the field to tackle him, Claude caught the ball, put it under his arm and sprang forward with a strength and speed which promised a magnificent gain. Willie Hardy, as it happened, was nearest to him and ran beside him to guard before the others could come upon the scene. But Claude was fast, and Willie was slow. Instead of running, Willie wobbled. One of his feet, which justice compels me to say were not large, got in front of the captain before he had gone five yards. Claude went down and, while the right tackle of the Cen-

trals fell upon him, managed to roll two yards
further, where he was arrested on the line by
the united weight of both the Central guards.

A groan arose from the wearers of the white
and gold and blue. Claude held the ball, it is
true, but he was downed within twenty yards
of his own goal. It was a bad beginning.

"First down; five yards to gain!" called the
referee, and as he spoke, the opposing elevens
lined up for their first scrimmage, while the
Milwaukee sympathizers in a body declared
with great earnestness and in full resonant
tones:

> Rickety rax, kerax, kerax,
> Rickety rax, keroo;
> Whenever we try to buck the line
> We go right through!

It was a mouth-filling yell, one of the most
satisfactory ever uttered in the city of Milwaukee. Some enthusiasts declared that by the
judicious use of this cry a dinnerless man could
go on to supper time without inconvenience.

"18, 15, 5, 28!" called Archer in a voice so
clear and distinct that it penetrated to the
furthest limit of the field.

"What does that mean, Mr. Elmwood?"
Mary Dale inquired.

While Elmwood was explaining, the play took

place. But in order to understand more clearly the game of football, it may be well to say something about signals. Before the ball is snapped back, it is necessary that the quarterback should know to what particular player he must pass it. It is necessary, moreover, that the man who receives it should know that it is coming to him and also in what direction he is to carry it. Furthermore, every player on the eleven must be ready to assist in the play. Of the rushers, some must block their man; occasionally all must block their man. When the opposing line is to be hit for a gain, the rushers must know just where the runner is coming, and those who are stationed at that part of the line must try to crowd back the forwards of the other side so as to make an opening. Hence, it is of the last importance that some sign or signal should be given which, while leaving the other side in ignorance, should enlighten every man on the offensive team as to who is to carry the ball and whither he intends carrying it. These signs may be given by gestures, by words or by numbers. As a rule, numbers are chosen.

The Milwaukee team, save for a few peculiar plays, used numbers. The following diagram will, with the appended explanation, give an idea of their meaning:

Left End	Left Tackle	Left Guard	Center	Right Guard	Right Tackle	Right End	
25	3	7	11	2	6	10	26
Collins 1	Hardy 5	Stein 9	Pierson 13	Drew 4	O'Rourke 8	O'Neil 12	

Quarterback
Archer 14

L. Halfback   R. Halfback
Dockery 15   Lightfoot 18

Fullback
Desmond 22

Each member of the eleven, as the diagram shows, has a number. Collins, for instance, is number one; Lightfoot, number eighteen; Stein, number nine, etc. Again, each space between the players in the rush line and around the ends has a number. Suppose now that the halfback called out for number fifteen to carry the ball in direction twenty-five. This would mean that Dan Dockery was to take the ball around the left end. On hearing this signal, every man on the team would know exactly what he was to do: some would spring forward, with the passing of the ball, to guard Dockery; others would block their men; others, it might be, if there were a previous arrangement to that effect, would make a feint of running in a different direction, so as to divert the attention of the opposing team from the real play.

In using this system of signals, the Milwaukee eleven conveyed their intended play by the second and third numbers. The first had no meaning, as also all that came after the third.

Supposing then that the quarterback were to call out 5, 22, 13, 17, 19, 20: the first number, 5, would count for nothing; the second, 22, would call for Maurice Desmond; and the third, 13, would admonish the team that Maurice was to make his way between the center rush and right guard of his own team and through the center and left guard of the opposing eleven. It would then be the duty of Maurice's center and right guard to make an opening by forcing back their opponents or crowding them aside. Other members of the Milwaukee team would try to hold their respective opponents so as to prevent them from interfering with the intended play, while others would rush before Desmond to make the opening doubly sure, or, as might be, would come after him to shove and push him through the line.

So, when Archer called out 18, 15, 5, 28, the number 18, as being the first, meant nothing; 15 called upon Dan Dockery to carry the ball; 5 signified that he was to go through the right tackle and right guard of the opposing line, and, in consequence, that Willie Hardy, our left tackle, and Stein, our left guard, were to try to force an opening for his passage. This was all that the signal itself conveyed, but a great deal more was implied. For this particular play, every man on the team knew just what he was expected to do. A blunder or bit of carelessness on the part of anyone might bring the attempt to naught.

As it is foreign to my purpose, and indeed would be almost impossible, to tell what each man was expected to do in accordance with pre-arrangement for each particular signal, I shall content myself with explaining what the players understood by this first signal of the game. *Ex uno, disce omnes.*

Dockery, then, is to receive the ball and plunge through the opening between the right tackle and right guard of the other side. He makes no motion to show that he is to get the ball; the quarterback, giving no sign that will enlighten the Centrals, bends down to receive the ball, and with open hands stands ready to catch it and to transfer it to Dockery. Meanwhile, the Milwaukee backs behind the line are standing with their hands on their knees and their heads bent low, waiting for the center to snap it back. As soon as he does so, Dan Dockery, Maurice Desmond and Claude dash forward at full speed— Dockery in the lead and with his head down,

the other two close behind and erect. As Dan
nears the line, the quarter passes it to him
in such a way that without effort he clasps
it to his stomach and goes on without pause
to the line, while Desmond and Lightfoot follow behind and push him with all their force
as he reaches the place where the opponents
are or ought to be. The quarterback helps
them to push.

Thus far we have accounted for six men
of the entire eleven. There are five others
who have their distinct work. No sooner is
the ball snapped back by the center rush
than the two ends, Collins and O'Neil, and
the right tackle, O'Rourke, start off at once.
The left end dashes into the first man behind
the line so as to clear the way, while the
right tackle and right end run on in the lead
of Dockery to interfere for him, provided that
he gets safely through the line. Meanwhile,
the center and right guard, the only two
positions not thus far accounted for, block
their opponents.

The uninitiated spectator, looking upon a
play like this—which, by the way, is one of
the simplest and most ordinary methods of
gaining ground through the line—may see
nothing but apparent confusion. He will
notice two or three men running up the field,

apparently to no purpose, and a compact crowd at the center of the line pushing and struggling without sign of purpose or order. Things, especially in football, are not what they seem.

Thus far, I have described this first scrimmage as it ought to take place—as it had been designed and studied and practiced. But we must remember that eleven men on the other side are to use every effort to spoil the play. The rushers will try to break through our line, the backs will strengthen their attack, and several of the opposing eleven will rush around the ends to break up the interference and tackle the runner. It will be seen, then, that a play like this depends for its success upon many circumstances.

Now here is what actually happened. The signal was given; for a moment there was a solemn pause. Then our center, who had been holding the ball lying sidewise upon the ground, rolled it back; whereupon a mighty wave of movement swept up and down both lines, for twenty-two players were now in action. As the quarter received the ball, he passed it without delay to Dockery, who, followed by Claude and Desmond, came swinging toward the place where the opening was to be forced.

And a fine opening was indeed effected, but it was made by the wrong men; for Willie Hardy, almost as soon as the ball was snapped, went flying back as though he had been struck by an elephant, and through the opening dashed Fox, the right tackle of the Centrals, and, behind him, their quarterback. While the former broke the interference, the latter tackled Dan and, assisted by one of his endmen and his halfback, brought Dockery down just one yard behind the place where the ball had gone into play.

"Second down; six yards to gain!" shouted the referee.

Then the wearers of the crimson in all quarters of the field yelled and hurrahed, while the students of the Central High School gave their pyrotechnical school-cry.

> Razzle dazzle
> Sizzle sazzle
> Zis—boom—bah;
> Central High School
> Rah—rah—rah!

"We shall have to give up that spot," whispered Claude to Harry.

"Yes; I made a mistake in beginning on that side. Hardy will spoil all our plays there, I'm afraid."

Seawell of the High School team was a brainy player. He surmised that the plays would be directed hereafter against the other side of the line and ordered his backs to prepare for the defense accordingly.

"There!" exclaimed Elmwood angrily. "Every man on the team did his work with a vim and a snap which would have brought the ball up the field at least five yards, if Hardy had even blocked his man."

"Why, where's all the slugging that I hear about?" asked the fair Mandolin, looking disappointed.

"Slugging is not allowed," Frank replied. "And not only that, but the men whose side have the ball cannot even use their hands, with the single exception of the runner, who may use the arm and the open hand to ward off tacklers. Sometimes, rarely though, a gentlemanly player may lose his temper and strike, but in so far he is an unfair player."

"Boys that act that way must be rowdies," said Mandolin virtuously.

"They betray a want of self-control, sometimes under circumstances where self-control would be heroic. But I think that, as a rule, such blows, given without malice and almost involuntarily, are not quite so bad as the blows which young gentlemen and young ladies inflict on one another by unkind words spoken in cold blood."

Mandolin thought it time to watch the game.

Both teams were in leash, as it were, till the center should snap back the ball as a preliminary to carrying out the following signal:

"17, 180, 60."

The first number, as has been said, meant nothing; the second, 18 (disguised by the addition of a zero), called for Claude; and the third, 6, disguised in the same way, bade him carry the ball between Drew and O'Rourke. This play, it will be seen, is precisely the same as the first but transferred to the other side of the line, and with a different man carrying the ball.

Claude, however, varied the play somewhat. Standing well back of the line, he started at a run before the ball was snapped back so as to get the maximum of speed. Pierson, the center rush, who knew Claude's play, instead of holding the ball lying sidewise on the ground, supported it on the small end and, in lieu of rolling it back, which is the slower but less difficult method, sent it into the air. The quarter caught it and dropped it into Claude's hands as he shot past. The way was not perfectly open for the captain. Drew held his man a little toward the center, but Gerald's vis-à-vis threw himself so low that there was no moving him. Gerald was quick at seeing an opportunity; he helped his opponent to get lower by holding him down, and Claude, with a pretty leap, went over him and through the line. In an instant, and while the backs who were to push Claude were falling heavily upon the man who had gone too low, the quarterback of the Centrals was clinging to Claude's waist. Claude, who had changed the position of the ball, bringing it under his left arm, shook him off with one of his unspeakable wriggles and ran into the arms of the left end, who had come back for him.

Then there ensued a movement which looked now like a waltz, now like a two-step. Claude, in the embrace of the end, whirled to one side for one yard, plunged forward for another, and was about to whirl again, when the right half came to the end's assistance and brought him down. But the play was by no means finished. Bracing himself on his knees, Claude, with the ball in his hands, reached forward full length for another yard's gain. Then Seawell pushed our captain's head into the earth and held him while the referee's whistle sounded for a down.

Claude had made seven yards.

There was much shouting, and the blasts of horns rang out, while the small boys of Milwaukee College waited their chance for being heard and, then, unable to control their impatience, made the following address in perfect and sonorous unison:

One, two, three, four, five, six, seven,
We're Milwaukee's crack eleven!
Eleven and ten, and eight and nine—
How we smash right through the line!

For the moment, the wearers of the crimson seemed to admit the justice of this declaration.

"Oh!" cried Mary Dale, "wasn't that mean! Did you see that big fellow pushing Claude's head into the ground?"

"When I grow up, I'll lick him," said the youngest Lightfoot thoughtfully.

"Pardon me, but there was nothing at all mean in the play, Miss Dale," said Frank. "Claude would do the same thing, if one of his opponents were, after being brought down, to squirm on the ground for further gains. There's nothing brutal about it either, the way Seawell did it. It looks bad, but really Claude was no more hurt by it than if he were wearing a wooden head. Don't you see that noseguard he has on? It protects the only part of the face that is at all sensitive in such plays."

"First down; five yards to gain!" cried the referee.

"Why, he said 'Second down, six yards to gain,' last time," objected Mary. "Why doesn't he call third down now?"

"Oh, I know that myself," said Alice. "They made their five yards and something more in that play and now they begin over again. Just as soon as a side has made its five yards, it starts off again with three more trials to make another five yards in."

"18, 150 [15], 10!" cried Archer.

Translated, these numbers mean that Dockery was to go between O'Neil and O'Rourke.

The ball was snapped, and the quarter threw it to Dockery. Even as Dan caught it, the tackle opposing Hardy sprang through as though there was no one there and, hurling Dan back for three yards, brought him heavily to the ground.

"Second down; eight yards to gain."

The Milwaukees lined up quickly; the signal was given for Maurice Desmond to go through the center. But Hardy was not prepared, and, again Fox, the fierce tackle, blocked the play.

"Third down; eight yards to gain."

"Can't you possibly hold your man?" inquired Claude of Willie.

"Yeth, I can; but he goeth through Collinth."

"If you don't get down low, instead of standing and allowing them to swing you anywhere they please, we might as well give up. Play like a man."

The team had now lined up.

"Get down low, Hardy!" bawled Claude. "Lower still; that's better!"

"17, 22, play low!" cried Archer.

"Play low" meant that the ball was to be kicked. The Milwaukees, despairing of making eight yards, had resolved to let their opponents have it—well up, however, on the Centrals' side of the field.

As the ball was snapped back, Archer with a full-arm movement sent it whirling to Desmond far behind. It was a splendid pass, one of the kind which had made Harry famous as a quarterback.

Although the redoubtable tackle of the Centrals broke through the line, followed by the quarter and the halfback, Desmond had plenty of time to kick. Claude and Dockery and Archer blocked the rushers who were in the advance, while Desmond, as he threw the ball slightly forward, caught it sharply in the hollow of his foot and sent it down the field some fifteen yards beyond the line in the center.

Seawell, anticipating the kick, had hastened back, but was too late to catch the oval on the fly. He succeeded in getting it, however, on the first bound, and turning quickly darted with splendid interference up the field.

Archer was the first of our side to follow the ball. Running at full speed, he scattered the interference like chaff, while Lightfoot, close behind, tacked the runner hard and low.

"Down!" yelled Seawell.

He arose, rubbing his shoulder, having brought the ball within one yard of the center of the field.

While the referee announced, "First down; five yards to gain," the Milwaukee senior students raising their voices above the shouting and horn-tooting of the crimson wearers made the following grave comment to the time of a stately march:

> Hark, hark, hark, O hark—!
> Archer always hits the mark!

The Centrals were fresh and in a hurry.

Our team accordingly had scarcely lined up, when the ball was snapped, passed to Seawell, who, preceded by three men, made straight at Hardy. That young gentleman might as well have been in the heart of Africa; and while Archer, who had run up to brace Willie, disposed of the first two men, the third, followed by Seawell, broke through the line. Dockery was blocked by the leader, Seawell warded off Lightfoot with his free hand and went on alone (for Dockery had detained his man) into what would have been a clean field were it not for Desmond who stood back of the line some twenty odd yards. Desmond made forward to tackle the Central's powerful captain, but was thrown off easily; and a groan arose from the sympathizers of the Milwaukee College.

The groan was almost instantaneously succeeded by a shout of hope.

"Lightfoot! Lightfoot!"

For Claude, putting on the speed which made him the fastest amateur sprinter in the Cream City, was already close upon the runner; and Seawell, who had lost something of his headway in getting away from Desmond, was brought to the ground a few seconds later after making a gain of about twenty yards.

"Halloa!" cried Frank, as he noticed a crowd of the players gathered in a knot at the center of the field, "somebody's hurt!"

"Where's Harry?" cried Alice in great excitement.

"Oh, he's all right," answered Elmwood. "I see him standing in the crowd."

Mandolin gave a little self-conscious shriek of dismay.

"Oh!" she cried turning up her lovely eyes till the whites were fully in evidence, "I do believe it's Willie Hardy."

"I hope it is," said Frank under his breath.

Strange to say, Mandolin was correct in her surmise. Willie it was, who with closed eyes lay upon the field. Insofar as he appeared to the sight, he gave every indication of being unconscious. But Dockery, who knelt beside him, could hear his heavy breathing.

"Get back!" yelled Dan, "get back, can't you, let him get some air! I think we had better bring out a substitute."

At this Willie opened his eyes and arose.

"I lotht my wind," he explained. "I played low, and they all trampled over me tho that I couldn't breathe. Now, I'm all right."

Meanwhile the delighted followers of the Centrals were rejoicing with brazen mouths and iron lungs. The "Razzle Dazzle" cry was given over and over. Then a young man with a voice which carried above horn and shout asked the following question:

"What's the matter with Seawell?"

"He's all right!" came the multitudinous answer.

But the inquisitive young man with the powerful voice was not satisfied.

"Who's all right?" he persisted.

"Seawell!" yelled the modern Greek chorus.

Then the young man made the following apostrophe:

"Isn't he a lallah!"

To which the chorus in tones of supreme satisfaction answered in linked sweetness a long, drawn out:

"Ah—h—h—h—h!!!"

The Milwaukee eleven were now somewhat demoralized. In the next scrimmage, the Centrals' right halfback made five yards through Hardy. Seawell carried the ball around the end for fifteen yards—of course on the most demoralized side of the team. Then, the left halfback, by way of variety, tried to go around the other end, but Archer was on him with the spring of a tiger, and tackling him brought him backward to the ground, where he continued rolling him for ten feet more.

"Second down; eight and a half yards to gain!" cried the referee.

Willie Hardy was the only player of the Milwaukees who looked at all winded. He was breathing heavily and was very pale. The rough usage was beginning to tell on him.

"Are you sick at the stomach?" asked Archer.

"No," said Willie. But the question gave him a bright idea. He had concluded during the last scrimmage that it would be more enjoyable to look on.

In the next play, Seawell went around the end for what would have been twelve yards had not Claude recovered some of the ground lost by throwing him back heavily at least six feet. Then, the right tackle of the Centrals came to the left and crashed into Willie with the result that the Centrals were within twenty-five yards of our goal.

Willie's quickness in going down, it had been noticed by competent critics, was inversely proportional to his alacrity in getting up. This time he stayed down with his beautiful eyes raised toward the blue and cloudless heavens.

"I'm thick," he gasped. "I feel ath if I wath going to die—or to faint."

The anti-climax aroused no smile; but the declaration of sickness did.

"Sick!" exclaimed Dockery. "Well, it's about time!"

Dockery felt sorry for the remark as soon as it was made. The others restrained themselves from expressing their sentiments, but I am bound to say that the faces of nearly every player on the Milwaukee eleven expressed a satisfaction which their owners were powerless to conceal.

And indeed had it not been for Mr. Keenan, Willie would have been kept out of the game from the start. Claude had wished to play George Hastings as tackle.

"I should like to allow it, Claude," Mr. Keenan had answered. "But I doubt whether we should use George Hastings at all. He is so light that there is danger of his being injured. If anyone gives out, we have no alternative but to use him. But, meantime, we shall have to take our eleven as it is."

However, when Willie was led off the field, supported by Dockery and Pierson, Claude beckoned to Hastings.

Then the small boys of Milwaukee College, whose acknowledged leader was Hastings, gave loose to their feelings of delight in the following apocalyptic language:

Hiki hiki—hai—kai
Muki mori—hai—yai!
To my mori
To my dori
Muki mori—hai—yai!

Becoming a shade more intelligible, they added:

Hoya, hoya saxa
Hoya, hoya saxa
Hastings!

The grown portion of the audience—using the vernacular, however—joined in these expressions of sympathy and enthusiasm, for the tender youth and lightness and modesty of the new player won them over at once.

But the change did not by any means fully remedy the weakness of the line. Fox, the heavy tackle opposing Hastings, forced him back in the ensuing scrimmage, and the runner made three yards. This run was followed by another for three, and another for six. The first and the third were between Hastings and Stein, and the second between Hastings and O'Neil. The prospects were getting worse and worse. Finally, after ten minutes of hard play, the Centrals had succeeded in bringing the ball up to within fifteen yards of our goal line.

Claude then exchanged a few hasty words
with Hastings. The boy nodded his head intel-
ligently and fell into the line for the next play.

Just after the signal was called, Hastings
quietly stepped back, and Claude as quietly
stepped into the vacated position. As the ball
was snapped, Fox, the opposing tackler, threw
himself with all his force upon the opposing
tackle. He intended, apparently, to crush
Hastings once and for all. But Hastings was
not there, and Claude, having helped the
astonished player on with a vicious forward
swing, darted through the line and was upon
Seawell before the Centrals could realize the
situation.

"Down!" roared Seawell as Claude forced
him backward.

It was well that he called so quickly; for
Claude, in the instant which succeeded the
cry, had brought him back three yards before
anyone could interfere.

"By Jove!" cried Elmwood in great excitement. "If Claude plays tackle, they'll never
get through that part of the line again."

"Halloa!" cried a man near the ropes, as
the teams again lined up, "Lightfoot is going
to play tackle instead of Hastings!"

The news spread quickly among the Milwaukee eleven's admirers, and aroused yells and blaring of trumpets and the waving of many canes and umbrellas. George Fox, the right tackle who had put Hardy out of the game and severely winded Hastings, looked fiercely at Claude. Fox was a powerful fellow, and just now he was flushed with confidence and victory. Much heavier than Claude, he had little doubt that he should be able to hold our captain at least three times out of five attempts.

Running behind the line, he approached Seawell.

"Say, Seawell," he said, "I think I can handle Lightfoot. Suppose you send the ball through him again. Take it yourself and get all the backs to guard you. If we make a good gain through Lightfoot, we'll completely demoralize the Milwaukees."

"All right," answered Seawell; and Fox returned to his position, where, drawing back a little, he gritted his teeth and prepared for a spring into which he was to put his every power to the strain. As the reader may remember, he could not, since his own side held the ball, use his hands; but his head and body were strong, and he was sure that Claude would be forced back.

The signal was given. The ball snapped

according to the slower but surer method, and while the Central backs clustered about Seawell, he received the ball and, closely guarded, made toward the line.

In the meantime, the twelve hundred spectators were treated to a most exhilarating sight.

At the moment that the ball was snapped back, Fox made a spring forward which was intended to knock Claude violently to one side. But Claude, who in watching Fox had surmised his intention, dropped low and, catching the springer's knees, gave him a lift which sent Fox flying into the air. Claude remained where he was, threw himself down just as the interference reached him, and while these players were sprawling over him, Archer, who had run around the left end, brought Seawell to the ground. Again the Centrals had lost instead of gaining.

"Third down; eight yards to gain," called the referee.

"Oh, I say!" yelled Eddie Coale, the mascot of the Milwaukees, "did you ever see a flying Fox? Isn't he a la-la?"

"Ah-h-h-h-h-h-h-h!" was the general answer.

The Centrals were now in possession of the ball on the eighteen-yard line and, as it happened, almost directly in front of our goal posts. They had but one more down, and in case they should fail to gain eight yards, the ball would be adjudged to the Milwaukees. It was a critical moment. The two teams were intensely excited, and the crowd realized that the next play was to be a critical point of the game. A stillness almost painful from contrast with the previous noise came over the field.

"18, 4, 177, 143!" called Seawell.

The ball was snapped, passed to the right half who went toward the left end, while the left back, the quarterback and the right tackle of the Centrals came rushing forward in the same direction. Seawell made on behind this group but rather slowly. Naturally, our team massed itself toward their opponents' left end, and while the scrimmage was growing hot and strong at that point, Seawell suddenly deflected in his course to the right and in front of our goal, while the ball was tossed toward him by the man who had made a feint of running with it.

Lightfoot and Archer were the first to notice the double pass and sprang from the melee toward the Central's captain. But while they were still running, Seawell suddenly dropped the ball and, as it rose from the earth, touched it lightly with his foot.

Then pandemonium ensued. The wearers of the crimson danced and shouted with joy that might be called frenzied; for Seawell had actually succeeded in kicking a goal from the field. It was a splendid play; and even Frank Elmwood could not but applaud.

"What has happened?" cried Mary.

"One of the prettiest plays on the grid-iron!" answered Frank enthusiastically. "Seawell was afraid of losing the ball on the third down and tried to kick a goal from the field. If he had failed, the ball would have gone to our boys, and they would be allowed to take it into play on the twenty-five yard line. But he has succeeded, and now the score is five to nothing. A goal kicked from the field counts five points."

"I knew we were going to be beaten," said Mandolin with much tranquility and resignation. "Willie Hardy told me so yesterday."

Frank endeavored to look polite.

"I hope Willie may turn out to be as good a prophet as he is a player," he said.

"He's not been a profit at all; he's been a loss," said Alice demurely.

This restored Frank's good humor and set Mandolin to thinking, which, I dare say, was a good thing for everyone in the party.

"Do you think the Milwaukee College eleven are going to lose?" continued Mary.

"I can't say yet," Frank made answer, passing his hand across his forehead. "I want to see what they can do when they get the ball. Their defensive play is now splendid."

"What do you mean by defensive play?"

"The kind of play they use when the other side has the ball. When our side has the ball, we play on the offensive."

"What are they going to do now?" Mandolin put in.

"They are going to start off in precisely the same way as they did in the beginning, except this time, the Milwaukees are going to have the kick-off."

The ball was placed in the center of the field. Claude tripped forward and sent it flying high and far down toward the right corner of the gridiron. The kick was remarkably good. Fox, standing on the five-yard line, caught it, but instead of running, waited for his men to come up. The pause was not long. Then, guarded by a wall of players, he started up the field.

"Goodness!" exclaimed Elmwood. "Those fellows are trained. As like as not they'll go fifty yards on that style of interference."

As the moving wall made forward and

gained its first few yards, Hastings met it at one end and was swept aside. O'Neil encountered the same fate as he ran up against the other end. Between these two and a little behind came Claude Lightfoot. And then ensued a play worthy of Mr. Heffelfinger. With a spring into the air, and planting his hand lightly on the middlemost of the defense, Claude shot clear over the moving wall and disappeared head foremost.

I said, a moment ago, that pandemonium ensued after Seawell's goal kicked from the field. What now followed was more than pandemonium. It was pandemonium with Babel and Babylon at their worst thrown in. Grave old men got upon their seats and danced and shouted. One venerable gentleman dashed his spectacles upon the ground and had to depend upon the testimony of his friends as to what happened for the rest of the game. Elmwood found that he was shaking hands with men whom he had never met in his life. Mary Dale blushed to find herself shouting and then noticed with supreme satisfaction that Alice was lifting up her voice too. The ropes which held off the spectators were broken at three different parts of the field, and the gridiron was at once alive with a mob of shouting, yelling, screeching, dancing maniacs.

Young Lightfoot tumbled over the grandstand and, although it was a fall of ten feet, kept on yelling, and put off the examination of his bruises to a quieter and less exciting moment.

Hardly a person on the field had seen Claude after he leaped over the line of defense. But they knew that the moving wall had become useless; and they heard—that is those who were in a condition to hear anything—that Claude had dropped squarely on Fox and brought him pinioned immovably to the earth six yards from the place whence he had started.

In clearing the field, seven Milwaukee policemen had an opportunity for ten most exasperating minutes of learning what a really exciting game of football is. Order was at length restored, and play was resumed with the ball in the possession of the Centrals exactly fifteen feet from the corner of their goal line. The signal was called, and the Central quarterback was just reaching for the ball which was rolling toward him from the center, when Drew, our guard, taking advantage of the wide-spread legs of his opponent, dived through and fell on the oval. Everybody available for the purpose on the Central side fell on Drew.

The referee whistled, and he and the umpire began to pull the mass of fallen players apart. Presently they discovered Drew, crushed yet happy, lying upon the ball, which he was affectionately clasping to his valiant bosom.

Of course, there was a wrangle. Seawell insisted that the ball had not been put into play, that Drew had seized it before the center rush snapped it back. Probably he believed so, but the referee had seen the play and adjudged the ball to the Milwaukees.

"Milwaukee's ball; first down; five yards to gain."

"17, 18, 11, 12, 13!" cried Archer.

The number 18 called for Hastings; 11 ordered him to go between Stein and Pierson.

Hastings caught the ball nicely and, with Archer at his left and Dockery at his right, made straight for the opening. But the opposing guard and center were down on their knees and immovable; Harry was rushing into a blind alley.

It will be remembered that Hastings was very light; Dockery and Archer kept this well in mind.

"Jump!" hissed Archer in George's ear.

As the lad leaped at the word into the air, the two gave him a lift and a swing which sent him clear over the line and forward into the right halfback's arms.

"Down!" shouted Hastings on the instant. The right halfback was strong and heavy and would, in all probability, have carried Hastings back to the line. As it was, George, the lightweight, had made five yards.

"First down; five yards to gain."

This time, Desmond took the ball and shot through the place well opened for him by Collins and Claude. Harry Archer was beside him on the side where he held the ball under his arm. He was tackled three feet beyond the line by the quarterback, but it was a high tackle, and Desmond at the time was plunging forward heavily.

Moving back a foot, Harry put his hand on the ball and, as Desmond still struggled with the tackler, snatched it from Maurice's arm and sped toward the goal line. It was but seven or eight yards away; there were but two minutes left before time was called, and Harry was determined to score.

"Good heavens!" yelled Frank. "Did you ever see such a sight?"

"Oh, dear!" cried Alice, putting her hands before her face. "Tell me if it is all right. I can't look."

To the spectators it seemed as though

Harry Archer were carrying the opposing eleven on his back. He shook off one, then another.

"Ah, he's down!" sighed Frank. "Hurrah, he's up again!"

For by some wondrous summoning of all his strength, Harry had struggled and staggered to his feet; and as he stumbled forward with four men hanging on to him, Claude Lightfoot dashed against him from behind with the seeming strength of ten. Four more of our players threw themselves against Claude, and with three opponents still clinging to him, Harry moved onward two feet and, making a supreme effort, threw himself forward and, reaching out with the ball, succeeded in placing it exactly on the goal line.

A deaf man would have heard the following remark:

> Rickety rax, kerax, kerax,
> Rickety rax, keroo;
> Whenever we try to buck the line
> We go right through!

Amid wild enthusiasm, Claude brought the ball out full thirty feet. Desmond, lying flat on the ground, held it till the captain was ready to kick. The ball was so far to one side of the goal that the kick was at a most difficult angle. No one, accordingly, was surprised when Claude missed the goal by a few feet, thus ending the first half with the score four to five in favor of the Central High School eleven.

Chapter XVI

IN WHICH ERNEST SNOWDEN SURPRISES EVERYBODY, AND THE GREAT FOOTBALL GAME COMES TO AN END

"COME here, Willie!" cried Mandolin Merry as Hardy, dressed in citizen's clothes, appeared in the grandstand.

"Thothe fellowth nearly killed me!" exclaimed Willie, as he seated himself beside the fair Mandolin.

"Are you hurt much?" she asked, while Mary and Alice gazed with more curiosity than sympathy, I am bound to say, upon the football hero.

"I think I am hurt infernally," answered Willie, meaning, doubtless, to say internally.

Frank was not with the party to remark that Willie had played infernally.

"Why did you stop, Willie?" pursued the society miss.

"Becauthe the whole Thentral team wath playing againtht me. They knew I came from Thaint Maureth." He added proudly, "Thaint Maureth ith the home of the football player."

"It was real mean," said Mandolin with a studied pout.

"Yeth, it wath," rejoined Willie. "But if it hadn't been for me, Claude Lightfoot would never have been able to raithe that tackle in the air the way he did. You thee, I winded that tackle; and when I left I knew he would be eathy to go againth."

"It was very brave of you to hold your own the way you did," continued Mandolin.

Alice and Mary turned away their heads.

"We are all brave at Thaint Maureth," said Willie with much simplicity. "The team at Thaint Maureth could beat both of thethe teamth put together."

"Do they play your style of game out there, Willie?" inquired Alice solemnly.

"Yeth, they do. And they know more trickth than thethe teamth ever read of."

Willie then kept Mandolin's sparkling eyes at their widest with narrations of the plays which he himself had suggested and carried out at "Thaint Maureth." He ended with informing his auditors that it was he who had trained Claude to jump over the line of defense and thus tackle the runner.

By the time he had come to a pause, Mandolin fairly worshiped him; and, upon my word, I think it was the fitting thing on the part of that young lady.

In a retired corner of the field, Frank Elmwood and Mr. Keenan were heartily shaking hands with the eleven.

"You are doing splendidly!" said Frank warmly. "Every man of you is doing his work. Now that Claude is at tackle, you have a line that any football team would respect."

"Don't give up, boys," added Mr. Keenan. "If you keep at it you have a splendid chance to win. But you will have to play hard; they have the lead, and they intend to keep it. What's the matter, Archer?"

"I don't know, sir; but I feel dead tired."

"You look pale, too. Here, give him a sweater and an overcoat. Now," continued Mr. Keenan, as he spread the coat on the ground, "lie down. You have to do a lot of work yet."

Archer lay down and closed his eyes. He looked thoroughly worn out. Though physically the strongest man on the team, stronger even than Claude, the want of training along with excessive study was telling upon him. Hastings, too, looked somewhat exhausted; he was in training, but was outclassed.

"I hope I'll be able to last out," said Harry Archer. "If we lose at all, it will be all my fault. I think I hurt my back in making that touchdown."

The other players were extremely attentive to their exhausted quarterback. They had seen how, from beginning to end, he had played "like a tiger." In making the touchdown, Harry had shown grit and endurance comparable with Lightfoot's greatest achievements on the gridiron.

When time was called for the second half, all but Harry fell into their places with a spring and buoyancy which showed what training is capable of.

"After everything has been said, I think it is a cruel game," Alice remarked to Frank, as he returned to his place beside them.

"Suppose," said Frank, "that I were to take a college boy just come from school, and set him to plowing on a broiling hot day. What would you say to that?"

"It would be downright cruelty," answered Alice.

"Precisely; it might injure him for life. And

why? Because he is not seasoned for that kind of work. On the other hand, if I were to put a farmhand at the same work on the same day, it would be all right. Now, take football. If you put men on a team who are not trained to fall, to tackle, to run, to guard, you are putting them in a position where they may be injured more or less seriously. To send a crowd of untrained men into the game would lead to cruelty. So it would be cruel to put a clerk at hard labor on the street. Football is a game that requires careful preparation on the part of those who are to engage in it. If people play it without that preparation they act unwisely. Nearly all the accidents and mishaps of football arise from the fact that boys undertake to play it who are utterly out of condition."

"What about Harry, then, Mr. Elmwood?" asked Alice anxiously.

Frank passed his hand over his brow.

"Well—he's—he's extremely strong, and he knows the game. But he's a little out of condition. I think, though, that he will come out all right. Halloa, there they begin again!"

Drew had just made the kick-off. The ball went low and straight to George Walker, the right halfback of the Centrals, who was standing on the twenty-five-yard line. Walker was a famous kicker. He saw his chance, and before the teams fairly realized that the ball had reached his hands, he returned it with a powerful kick that sent it back to our fifteen-yard line and into the hands of Harry Archer.

There is a fascinating and gruesome tale for children in Grimm's popular tales, entitled, I believe, "The Man who Wanted to Know what Shivering Meant." A pretty story might be attempted on similar lines of a boy who wanted to know how a man felt when he was frightened. The boy-hero might stop a runaway horse, capture a train robber and still cry out, "Oh, if I only knew what it was to be frightened!" Finally, after all manner of hair-breadth escapes, he would be placed, by the author, on the gridiron; and the ball, at the kick-off, would come slowly but surely straight toward him. Hereupon this hero of a hundred adventures would rush from the field, crying as he went, "Oh! At last I know what it means to be frightened!"

Seriously, the most nerve-trying moment for any player arrives when the ball is coming toward him high through the air. Harry Archer had never before known what it was to have "nerves" on the gridiron. But now he knew it with a vengeance. There was the ball coming, oh, so slowly, as it seemed to him, and rushing down the field like savage demons came ten of the Centrals! He fancied that each one of those men was bent on striking him with all his strength, with all the momentum of his run, flat to the earth. They looked to him like giants; they seemed to be not ten but a hundred. A sickening feeling came over him. He shivered and, for perhaps the first time in his life, was thoroughly frightened. But there was no escape. Nearer and nearer came the ball. How big it looked. It touched his hands.

Harry, to the surprise of all the spectators and the dismay of many, dropped it. Gerald O'Rourke picked it up and started to run; but before he had made three strides, the Central halfback brought him to the ground; and so the scrimmage of this second half began with the ball a little on the wrong side of our twenty-five yard line.

The ball was then advanced by our players on rushes through the line for forty yards, when it was lost on three downs. The Centrals brought it back ten yards, and lost it. The teams were now lined up in the center of the field.

Desmond hit Fox for five yards. Hastings, assisted by splendid interference on the part of Archer and Lightfoot, made fifteen yards around the end. Dockery broke through the opening made for him by Claude and Stein, and was downed after a gain of six and a half yards.

The Centrals were showing signs of fatigue. Though in excellent training, they were not so hardy as their opponents. In the next play, Claude, taking the ball on the left, ran to the other side and sped through between the tackle and the end. Claude had been having a comparatively easy time since the beginning of the half and was now at his best. Archer was beside him, and Collins had run on ahead to attend to Seawell.

As Claude went through the line, he dashed against the left half and, springing away from him like a ball of rubber from the wall, he spoiled the end man's chance to tackle him by a powerful sweep of his left hand, which brought his opponent down. Archer meanwhile jogged the Central's quarterback to one side, and now there was a clean field, provided the fullback could be avoided.

While Archer, then, was delayed in blocking the quarterback, Claude, alone, started at a wide angle, running toward the goal line and away from the fullback. It was a race between the two captains having for its objective point the extreme corner of the goal line, toward which Seawell was taking the shortest distance by several yards.

But Claude was going at full speed; he had, as it were, the advantage of a "flying start" over his opponent, and the sympathizers with the Milwaukees were already shouting the cry of victory.

"Eight to five!" roared a man above the din. As his voice broke the air, Claude's right foot caught in a small hole, and down he went with a violence which should have stretched him senseless. It did not, however, but it entailed what was, in Claude's judgment, a worse misfortune. The ball slipped from his grasp and rolled, as luck would have it, toward Seawell, who picked it up quickly and brought it twenty-five yards up the field before he was successfully tackled by O'Rourke.

"Isn't that hard luck!" cried Frank Elmwood. "We've lost the game by a fluke."

"A what?" asked Mary.

"A fluke—a mischance. If the field had been all right, Claude would have made a touchdown, and the score would now be eight to five in our favor."

"If Claude knew the firtht printhiples of football," observed Willie, with a sage nod of his head, "he would have held on to the ball. At Thaint Maureth, they would ecthpell a boy from the college for thutch a play ath that."

The Centrals began to play an extremely cautious game. Avoiding the vicinity of Claude, they hit the line repeatedly, making gains of one, two and three yards. Realizing that they now had the victory in their hands, provided they could hold out for ten minutes longer, they worked with a new access of energy.

Harry Archer, as has been said over and over again, was a wondrously good quarterback. One of the secrets of his success was that he made a careful study of the faces and positions of his opponents. Throughout the game, he had watched and pondered; light came gradually. He found out during this stage of the game that the quarterback of the Centrals changed his position for several plays. When the ball had been brought up, slowly but surely, by the Centrals, five yards beyond the middle of the field, Archer could make out for several different plays who was to take the ball and whither the runner was to go. After one of the scrimmages, he managed to convey the fruits of his observation to Claude.

"Good!" said Claude. "I'll engage to stop the

back on my side, if you look out for the other one. Both of us will attend to the fullback."

Harry stationed himself between the right tackle and end. The signal was announced, and he saw from the quarter's pose that the left half was to take it. When the ball was snapped, he broke through and was on the halfback as he caught the ball. As the half-back had not had time to put on speed, Harry wisely tackled him high, and brought him down and back with a loss of five yards.

In the next scrimmage, Seawell made one yard through the center.

"Third down; nine yards to gain."

Desmond, our fullback, anticipating a kick, ran far down toward his goal. Archer stationed himself behind Lightfoot at tackle.

The ball was snapped back. So was Fox, and as Claude followed by Archer dashed through the opening, the Central's quarter made a long pass to Seawell. The pass was not of the best, and Seawell fumbled it. Abandoning his idea of kicking the ball, he jumped to one side of Claude and made toward the end. Archer sprang at him and just succeeded in holding him for a moment. Seawell went another yard or two when Collins tackled him fast. The Centrals had failed in making their five yards.

"Milwaukee's ball; first down; five yards to gain."

The teams were now lined up near the middle of the field. The crisis of the game had come. Should the Milwaukees lose the ball, they were to all intents and purposes defeated. Little time was left, and fifty-five yards were to be made.

"Don't waste a second!" said Claude to Harry.

To begin with, Hastings made a run around the end and, in the excitement of the moment, got away from his interference on a clear field. Seawell made at him in a terrible dash and brought him to the ground with extreme violence.

The referee's whistle sounded, but George did not rise.

"Mark off time there!" cried Claude, running up to George's side.

George was dazed and hurt, and for some minutes there was a respite from the game which had now become "hot and furious."

"There!" exclaimed Alice, "that was brutal."

"I think not," said Frank. "Seawell tackled in the proper way, and tackled hard. But when one hundred and eighty pounds tackles ninety-five pounds properly, it's no wonder that the light-weight gets hurt. The fact of the matter is that George has no right to play in a regular eleven. He shouldn't be allowed."

And now there occurred an event which I set down with great pleasure.

Ernest Snowden, accompanied by Mr. Keenan, stepped onto the field and called Lightfoot aside.

"Look here, Claude," said Ernest, "I'm ashamed of myself for the way I've carried on, and I wish to apologize. I am a little late about it, but if you need my help, here I am."

Claude caught Snowden's hands in his.

"Oh, you're a bully fellow, Snowden! I'm so glad that we've made up. And I want to apologize for anything I did out of the way; if I ever bullied you, I didn't—"

"No, you never did."

"Claude," put in Mr. Keenan, "I cannot allow George Hastings to play any longer; it is now almost a matter of conscience with me."

"All right, sir! Run in and dress quick, Snowden. My, I feel good!"

Then Seawell stepped over and touched his hat to Mr. Keenan.

"I feel like a big bully," he said. "It makes me feel mean to hurt a little fellow, but I sincerely hope, Mr. Keenan, that you do not think I was intentionally rough."

"You were perfectly right, Seawell. We were to blame for putting so light a youngster on the field. As regards your tackling, I'm sure not a boy on our eleven thinks that you did anything that could be criticized."

"It's nice to play with gentlemen," said Seawell.

"That's what our side has been saying all along," rejoined Claude very neatly.

Hastings, meantime, had risen, and protested his willingness to continue playing.

"Shake hands," said Seawell heartily. "You don't feel any worse than I do."

"Oh, it was all in the game," said George smilingly. "And it was all my fault. If I had kept with my interference, probably I should not have been hurt at all."

"Well, George," said Claude, "we shall take no more risks on you till you've gone and insured your life. Ernest Snowden has offered to help us out in so generous a way that he has made me feel quite ashamed of myself. I've been guilty of rash judgment over and over today."

And Claude mentally resolved to go to Confession that very night.

Shortly after George Hastings had left the

field, slight, slender and pale, a new player, stout, powerful and fresh, bounded over the ropes.

" 'Rah for Snowden!" cried Claude.

The newcomer blushed, with some reason, as the crowd broke into cheers that were enthusiastic to the last echo.

Snowden had softened at the last moment. He had resisted Mr. Keenan's first overtures with obstinacy. But the prefect's attempt had not been wholly fruitless, for he had succeeded in bringing home to the recalcitrant player the fact that he had put himself utterly in the wrong. As the game went on, Snowden grew more and more ashamed of himself. He was thinking of going to Claude during the interval between the two halves and making some sort of apology, but pride held him back.

When, however, while Hastings lay stretched upon the field, Mr. Keenan again approached him, he swallowed his pride heroically and apologized with true humility. An act of this kind often changes a person's life. Snowden, it may be said in passing, was a better boy from that moment of self-conquest.

Before lining up, it was decided that Claude should play halfback and that the new recruit should attend to Fox, who, by the way, now that Claude was done with him, needed very little attention indeed. Poor Fox, having, like the proverbial month of March, come in like a lion, gave promise of going out like a lamb. Accordingly, when the teams fell into position, the Centrals were facing the strongest eleven that Milwaukee College had ever got together.

"Now we're going to have some fun!" cried Frank Elmwood, as he caught the signal. "We're going to have a double pass."

"What is that?" asked Mary Dale.

"Whenever the ball is put in play it must come from the center to the quarterback, and from him to some third man. Till it has reached a third man, the ball cannot be advanced. Now whenever the third man, instead of running with it, passes it back to a fourth man, you have what is called the double pass. In the present case, Harry Archer will pass the ball to Dan Dockery. Dan will go on a run toward the opposite side; Claude Lightfoot will run in the contrary direction to Dockery and, as he passes behind Dan, will receive the ball. There now, watch!"

For some reason or other, perhaps owing to the changes in position, several of our men failed to attend to the work assigned them in this particular play; and, in consequence, the interference which Claude looked for as Dan passed him the ball was not on time. On the instant, he decided to go forward alone. He began his progress by dashing into the end, who, still under the impression that Dockery had the ball, was trying to get around to tackle Dan, and rebounding from the shock, Claude sped onwards, sweeping away the quarterback with his hand and dashing full-tilt into the Central's left halfback. The usual dance ensued with the advantage decidedly to Claude's account. Seawell, however, despite Harry Archer's interference, brought the dance to a sudden end in throwing Claude violently to the ground and holding him fast.

The Milwaukees had counted on a run of twenty or thirty yards from this play. They were disappointed; though Claude, almost entirely by individual play, had made ten yards.

Before the next scrimmage took place, the linesman notified the two captains that but six minutes were left for play.

Captain Seawell received this news with elation; not so Claude. His side had the ball, it is true; but they were still distant forty-five yards from their opponents' goal line. To lose the ball on downs now meant to lose the game. To fail of making forty-five yards in six minutes would leave the score four to five in favor of the Centrals. In any event, no time was to be lost.

In the next three plays, five yards were gained.

"Forty yards to make," thought Claude, "and not more than two or three minutes."

"Watch out!" said Frank to the young ladies; "there's going to be a strange play now."

While the teams were lined up amid a tense silence, a low whistle sounded. Forthwith every player on the Milwaukee eleven, save the center rush, changed position with lightning-like rapidity. Archer took Dockery's place, stationing himself three or four yards outside of Dockery's usual position; Dockery took Lightfoot's place; Lightfoot Archer's, while the right end, right tackle and right guard changed places with the men on the left. Maurice Desmond, the fullback, went up almost to the rush line and stationed himself full twenty yards to the right of his end man. There he stood alone and solitary, the observed of all.

Here is the position of the Milwaukees after the changes had been effected:

O'Neil	O'Rourke	Drew	Pierson	Stein	Snowden	Collins	
L. E.	L. T.	L. G.	Center	R. G.	R. T.	R. E.	
O	O	O	O	O	O	O	
			O				Desmond
			Lightfoot				O
Archer					Dockery		
O					O		

The Centrals were certainly puzzled by these positions. What was Desmond doing over there?

"Get low, lower, boys!" cried Claude.

At these words, which were the signal, the ball was snapped back, while apparently every player of the Milwaukees made toward Desmond. Taking the cue from the Milwaukees, the Centrals made for the point where Desmond was stationed too. There was one exception, however. Archer turned quietly in the opposite direction, and Claude by a full-arm pass sent the ball into his arms as he rushed down into a clear field—clear, were it not that Seawell stood within twenty yards of his goal line waiting for the unexpected. Down the field flew Archer, five, ten, fifteen yards, while the air was filled with yell and cheer and shout. Down the field he dashed full twenty yards, and as Seawell dived at him low and viciously, Harry by a jump and swerve managed to escape in part. But Seawell had succeeded in catching him with one strong hand, and Harry, though not held, went down. He was up again in an instant, and Seawell was up and after him.

As Harry rose, the shout of triumph was ear-piercing. But twenty yards to gain, and a free field!

"Halloa!"

"What's the matter?"

"Is he hurt?"

A thousand anxious questions were put to unheeding ears, as Harry after making ten of the twenty yards, began to go slow, to stagger—

And there was Seawell dashing down on him like a whirlwind. Oh, but it was a painful moment for our boys! In an instant Seawell would be upon him—and then?

"Spurt! Spurt, Harry!" cried a dozen hearty voices, the owners of which were near the goal. "Spurt, Harry!"

As though awakened from a sleep, Harry, biting his lips, made a desperate endeavor, and just as Seawell leaped into the air to bring him down, he quickened his pace with a suddenness which threw the tackler out of his reckoning. Both came to the ground, but separate, and as Seawell reached forward desperately to hold the runner, Harry, by rolling over thrice, brought the ball safely into the goal-line.

He did not hear the yells that volleyed, the cries that rattled; he did not see the Milwaukee sympathizers in all their manifestations of extreme joy. Harry, with the ball under his arm and his face turned toward the sky, lay unconscious. He was carried off the field at once.

Claude kicked the goal easily, making the score ten to five in favor of Milwaukee College.

But one minute was left. Claude called in an indifferent substitute in place of Archer; Seawell kicked the ball from the center, and after the first scrimmage, time was called with the score ten to five in favor of Milwaukee College.

While the Milwaukee students, having taken possession of three Twelfth Street cars, were shouting their yells, cheering their players and indulging in all manner of vocal vivacity—there came a sudden silence.

An ambulance wagon was passing them; and they knew that in it lay Harry Archer unconscious, with Claude Lightfoot supporting the head of his friend.

Chapter XVII

*IN WHICH HARRY LEARNS THAT HE CANNOT
COMPETE IN THE MATHEMATICAL CONTEST*

HARRY was to go to work on the day following Thanksgiving, and on the next
Wednesday he was to compete for the Mathematical prize.

The doctor who examined him put an end
to these intentions. Unlike most men of his
profession, he was cross and unsympathetic.

"Oh! It's a football game, is it?" he said
with savage irony. "One ounce of pleasure to
five tons of pain. It is a sarcasm to call such
a thing a game. Football as now played is
a free-for-all-fight. It is a sport fitted only
for barbarians."

Poor Harry, as he lay white and stiff upon
his bed, could not help wondering whether
it would be possible for barbarians or even
semi-barbarians to play the game for two
minutes without diverting it into another
channel; but he said nothing.

"Madam," continued Doctor Rose, address-
ing Mrs. Archer after he had prodded and
pinched and sounded Harry's chest and back,
"I cannot find exactly where the injury is
as yet. Something is the matter with his

spinal column. It may, as like as not, result in paralysis," he added with fine brutality, "but I cannot tell yet. The boy must lie perfectly quiet for two or three days; and then, unless he improves, I shall put him in a plaster-of-paris jacket. Here's a prescription which I want you to have filled at once. Give the boy absolute rest. Give him a bread-and-water diet; that is what I should like to put every football player in the country on."

"Excuse me, Doctor Rose, but we did not call you in to scold our boy," said Mrs. Archer mildly.

"And we sent for you because we could not get our regular family doctor, who most unfortunately is absent," added Alice. "We did not want your services as a judge, but as a doctor."

"Probably you want someone else!" cried the physician, glaring at Alice.

"We intend to get another doctor as soon as possible," answered Mrs. Archer firmly.

And she paid Doctor Rose his fee as though she had untold wealth in reserve.

"That fellow is a bully," said Harry feebly. "I don't want any of his medicine. But I feel awfully bad that I can't get up. I'm afraid, Mother, that I shall have to stay in bed and lose my chance in the contest. I don't mind losing the situation so much, but I had set my heart on trying for that prize."

On the following day, Father Trainer visited Harry. The great mathematician, on seeing his best beloved pupil lying still and helpless on his back, pulled out his handkerchief and rubbed his eyes.

"Are you in pain, Harry?" he inquired.

"Very little, Father, except when I try to sit up; then my back hurts me awfully. What I feel most is that I can't go in for that contest."

"Are you sure, Harry?"

"Yes; the second doctor who came to see me yesterday afternoon says the same as the first doctor. He insists on my lying perfectly still and forbids me to take any other attitude for two weeks."

Father Trainer rubbed his eyes again.

"You have to make that competition, Harry."

"It's impossible, Father."

"There's no such word!" cried the Father. "Does the doctor know exactly what's the matter with your back?"

"No; he speaks of calling in one of the leading surgeons of the city for a conference."

Father Trainer's eyes brightened. "You haven't given permission yet, Mrs. Archer?"

"To tell you the truth, Father, we have not the money. Alice is trying to borrow something this morning."

"Good!" cried the mathematician. "Now do me a favor. Tell your doctor to wait one day, and the day after tomorrow I'll see you again. Do you understand?"

"Yes, Father Trainer," answered Mrs. Archer, "we shall be glad to do anything you suggest, for we appreciate far more than we can say your kindness to our boy."

Father Trainer arose hastily and, with an abruptness which was saved from being rude by the preoccupied air which had come upon him, made for the door.

"Oh, I beg pardon!" he said, stopping short. "Haven't you a vacant room in the house?"

"We have three, Father," answered Mrs. Archer with a slight flush.

"Now, I don't want to hurt your feelings," stammered the Father, "but—but—couldn't you do me a great favor by letting out one of your rooms to a dear friend of mine, a distant relation? The house is in a quiet neighborhood, and I think it will be just the thing for him."

"Indeed, Father, it is you who will do me a favor. I now see that it will be absolutely necessary for me to take a boarder or two, if we are to keep the house; and I know how hard it is to get desirable persons."

"Capital! Good-bye!"

And Father Trainer hurried away so absorbed that he took the wrong car and would not have paid his fare had not the conductor almost laid violent hands upon him. He did not discover his mistake in direction till he arrived at Wauwatosa. It took him over an hour to reach the college, which was not ten minutes' ride from the Archer's home.

On gaining his room, he dashed off the following letter:

MILWAUKEE COLLEGE
Nov. 28, 189—

DEAR AMBROSE: Your letter informing me that you wanted to get away from your practice to finish the work on nervous diseases, which you have been engaged upon for the last two years, reached me yesterday. You asked me whether I can get you a room in some quiet home. At first nothing occurred to me. But just now I made a great discovery. A dear pupil of mine, Harry Archer by name, was seriously hurt last Thursday, day before yesterday, in a football game. He is a splendid fellow, and he has the nicest mother and the best of sisters. They are very poor—though it is not commonly known in this city. They have rooms; their situation is retired, and it will be just the place to finish your book. Above all, I want you to come for the boy's sake. The two doctors who have examined him don't quite make out what's the matter with him. Now I am perfectly certain that you can cure him faster than any man I know of. You cured me after six doctors in the East washed their hands of me; and you must cure Harry. Now instead of delaying to come until Wednesday as you proposed, I want you to come at once. There is no time to be lost. My boy is entering a mathematical contest here—an account of which I send you, cut from the "Evening Wisconsin." He is a genius at mathematics and must carry the day. But he can't move, and the doctors are talking about paralysis. Please come. If you can't get off tomorrow, Sunday, come on Monday.

Remember me to Mrs. Kendall and all the little ones. Your sincere and grateful friend,

CHARLES TRAINER

DR. AMBROSE KENDALL
Lake Avenue, Chicago

At nightfall, Father Trainer received the following telegram:

Will arrive Monday at eleven. Meet me at depot.   AMBROSE KENDALL

Meanwhile, Harry was not neglected by his school friends. After class on Friday and Saturday, they came in crowds. Claude Lightfoot, in particular, was most attentive. He studied Harry and his wants. Flowers and dainties and books and magazines were showered upon the patient.

Willie Hardy was pleased to show his pretty face in the sick-room and asked Harry whether he would like to have a full set of *St. Nicholas*. Harry answered that nothing would please him better, whereupon Willie promised to bring them the next day. He did not keep his promise, however; but Claude, who was present, attended to the matter himself.

"I thay, Claude," said Willie, as the two left the house together, "it ith no uthe to be a piouth boy. Harry Archer wath the betht thudent in our clath; and his folkth are poor. And just when he geth a job, he ith hurt, and can't do anything. He had a chanth to win eighty dollarth too, and he wath praying for it, and the other fellowth were praying for him, and it dothen't do any good."

"Look here, Willie Hardy; you mustn't get everything wrong. When a boy prays for a temporal favor, he prays for it, or ought to pray for it, with the condition that he may gain it provided it is best for him. Some-

times when we pray for a temporal favor, it
may be that the gaining of it might make
us proud or vain, or in some way interfere
with what God knows to be best for our
souls."

"I thaw all that in the catechithm," said
Willie.

"Yes; but perhaps it has never come home
to you. You remember how it happened that
I was put off making my First Communion?"

"Yeth," said Willie. "You were not fit."

"Well, I had prayed hard and so did Kate.
And I was terribly disappointed when my
prayer, as I thought, was not heard. And
then when I did make my First Communion
I was awfully scared and frightened. But
since then, I have seen that everything happened for the best. Now even if poor Harry
Archer loses his chance for the prize and
his health, you have no right to say that
God did not hear his prayer. God sees further than we do; and what seems a misfortune may turn out to be the very best thing
that could happen."

"Whenever I pray," said modest Willie, "I
alwayth get what I athk for."

Claude was tempted to inquire whether
Willie ever prayed at all, but he checked himself and, "smiling passed the question by."

Chapter XVIII

*IN WHICH IT IS SHOWN THAT DOCTORS MAY
COMPARE FAVORABLY WITH EVEN THE
BEST OF MATHEMATICIANS*

TOWARD noon on the following Monday, Father Trainer and a stout gentleman somewhat under the middle height were following Mrs. Archer up the stairs.

"Now mind, Mrs. Archer," the stout gentleman was saying in a clear, ringing voice, "now mind, I'm not a surgeon. If your boy needs a surgeon, I won't be able to do much. But I sincerely trust that my diagnosis will discover that he doesn't need a surgeon at all. Did you pay that hackman, Father Trainer?—Oh, you did. And you're sure that both my valises are—Oh, I have one and you have the other."

Thus talking energetically, the great Dr. Kendall, nervous, fidgety, considered to be the best neurologist in the Northwest, entered Harry's room.

"So you are Harry Archer, and you've been playing football? Don't try to move, my boy. I'm sincerely sorry you got hurt. Now mind," he added, shaking his left index finger at Mrs. Archer, as he warmly clasped hands with the boy, "I don't want you to get a prejudice against football. I consider it one of the strongest and most encouraging revolts against the effeminate tendencies of this degenerate century."

Harry smiled gratefully and was in love with Doctor Kendall from that hour.

The neurologist stood for a moment looking fixedly at Harry. Then he took the chair which Mrs. Archer brought and, seating himself beside the bed, felt Harry's pulse.

"Who beat?" he said, looking intently at his watch.

"We did, sir, by a score of ten to five. I got hurt in making the last touchdown."

"Good! That's an encouraging symptom. If you had been beaten," here the doctor broke into a charming smile, "you would feel much worse than you do. My, what an arm you have! Come over here, Father Trainer, and feel this arm. A boy like you has no right to be in bed. Now, suppose you try to sit up."

Harry, not without difficulty, sat up in bed.

"I think there shall be no need of a surgeon, Mrs. Archer. That's right; lie down again. Where do you feel the pain?"

"In my back, sir."

"Is it a dull pain?"

"Yes, sir."

"And you don't know exactly where it is?"

"It seems to be all over."

"Yes, yes," the physician here pulled at his mustache again.

"Is there any danger of paralysis, sir?" asked Mrs. Archer, who was gazing upon the doctor as though he held in his hand the balance of life and death for her boy.

"I think not, Ma'am. But I shall know for certain in a few minutes. By the way, I hope you have given no offense to the other doctor on my account."

"No, sir; when we hesitated about letting him put Harry in a plaster-of-paris jacket before he could say what was really the matter with our boy, he was willing to wash his hands of the whole affair."

"When did you go to sleep last night?"

"About two, sir."

"Has it been that way for the last three or four weeks?"

"Nearly six weeks, sir."

"No, Mrs. Archer, we shan't need a surgeon at all. And hasn't your imagination been quite lively at night?"

"Yes, sir," answered Harry in astonishment. "It's been too lively for my taste."

"Oh, no, Mrs. Archer, there shall be no plaster-of-paris jacket. And were you studying much before going to bed?"

"Four and five hours, sir."

"And you couldn't get your studies out of your head when you lay down?"

"No, sir."

"And sometimes after going to sleep you would suddenly awake with a nervous jerk that seemed to begin at your great toe?"

"Yes, sir, it has happened every night lately. Sometimes seven or eight times a night."

"And you may have noticed that you have grown irritable of late—snappish, quick?"

"Indeed I have."

"I'm almost glad you played that game. Madam, there isn't the least danger of paralysis."

"But what about my back?"

"Oh, I'll fix that; that's only a symptom. The football game did not do you much harm."

"What!" cried Mrs. Archer.

"No, Madam. Your boy has been ill probably since the end of September or the beginning of October, and getting worse every day. He has simply overworked himself. The day he went in to play football, he was in no condition to do anything; he should have been in bed."

"I knew there was something wrong, but I didn't know I was sick," protested Harry.

"Probably you never were really ill in your life, young Hercules, and thought you would be acting the baby to take notice of want of sleep and a dozen other little irregularities which came upon you. You were hurt in that football game, but the game, as you philosophers say, Father Trainer, was rather the occasion than the cause. If you hadn't gone under in that game, it is very probable that your real complaint, which people call neurasthenia—though I am prepared to sustain a thesis to the effect that there's no such illness in the world—it is probable, I say, that concealment, like a worm in the bud, would have caused your sickness to develop so as to make you a confirmed invalid for several years, if not for life. As it is, I engage to cure you perfectly in six weeks."

Harry's eyes flashed joy; Mrs. Archer murmured a devout "Thank God"; but Father Trainer looked alarmed.

"O Ambrose!" he exclaimed, clasping his hands and coming forward, "this won't do at all. Six weeks! Why the boy must go down to the Public Library on Wednesday and go in for that contest."

"The boy must give up mathematics for three months. Now, I'm positive about that."

"He shan't!" cried Father Trainer.

"It's absolutely necessary."

"Well, let him give up mathematics; but he must make that contest!"

"He can't stand it, Father Charles."

"What are you a doctor for, Ambrose? You must make him stand it!"

"But, he's not able to sit up, and he won't be for at least a week."

Father Trainer sank back in his chair as though he had received his death warrant.

"Now mind, Father Trainer, I don't want to blame you in the least. But Harry Archer has been done almost to death with study. It has been all work and no play—isn't that so, Mrs. Archer?"

"It is my fault, doctor," said the mother.

"It's mine," cried the despondent mathematician.

"The blame is on myself, doctor," said Harry. "My mother has done her best without positively ordering me to keep me from my books after ten o'clock at night. And then I gave up exercise, and I used to be a big athlete."

"Well, you'll have to become a big athlete again. Once you are well, you must take plenty of exercise, and plenty of sleep, and then you can study hard too. It isn't the study that has hurt you exactly, but study out of proportion to recreation and to sleep."

The doctor now seated himself on the bed and put his arm under Harry.

"Suppose you tell me about that football game."

Harry began the account, and had reached the first down after the opening kick-off when he suddenly winced.

"Ah!" said the doctor. "I have found one of the spots where the pain is seated. Go on."

In the course of his narration, Harry winced three distinct times.

"There will be little trouble about the pain in the back. The first thing to do is to get you to sleep well and put your nerves in order. We shall start at that at once. Then tomorrow I am going to burn you."

"I beg your pardon, sir?"

"Burn you on the back; you won't mind it. No football player would. It will take the pain away very soon, and you'll be about in a week. But you mustn't study or exert yourself in any way whether by running or jumping or even walking, for two, or possibly three months."

"I am to live the life of a vegetable?"

"Well, yes; however, you may do a little light reading every day—but none after nine o'clock at night."

"That's fine!" cried Harry. "I have neglected reading all my life, and now I can make up for lost time."

"But, doctor, can't you burn him today?" cried Father Trainer eagerly. "Fix him up so that he can attend that contest."

"Why, he'd be too sore on Wednesday to move if I did so."

"Then you shan't burn him tomorrow either, Ambrose."

"Why not?" And the physician turned a despairing look upon Mrs. Archer and added, "See how he lords it over me."

"Because he's going into that contest," answered Father Trainer firmly.

"Bother the contest!"

"I am bothering about it; and Harry must make it."

The doctor laughed, and taking out his prescription tablet became suddenly grave. He wrote slowly and then read to himself three distinct times what he had written. Tearing off the slip, he handed it to Mrs. Archer and proceeded to write another prescription, which as before he read thrice.

"There," he said. "Get these filled, and take them strictly according to the times prescribed."

He then gave at length further directions

to Mrs. Archer, and when he departed, Harry and his mother, deprived of his genial presence, felt as though the sun had gone behind a cloud.

"O Mother, isn't it good! Poor Claude Lightfoot has been so distressed and thinks that he is the cause of my being hurt. It will relieve him so when I tell him what the doctor said. Isn't he a wonderful man? Why in five minutes he told me everything queer about myself that's happened in six weeks. The other doctors didn't ask me such questions at all; and I didn't think for a moment that my sleeplessness and touchiness had anything to do with the matter."

"He is a great doctor, Harry. How kind it was of Father Trainer to get him for us. People in the Far East often pay Doctor Kendall tremendous fees simply to come and make a diagnosis of their trouble. He is going to stay with us, treat you for nothing, and insists on paying his board. O my boy, I am so grateful to God!"

"How about the mortgage, Mother?"

"I trust in God for that too. He has been so good to us that we would be ungrateful to give up yet."

The doorbell rang, and Mrs. Archer left the room. When she returned, there was a glad smile upon her face.

"Look, Harry!" she exclaimed, handing him a telegram.

> Don't sell silver shares. There is hope yet.
>
> JAMES STONE

"O Harry!"

And Mrs. Archer put her head beside her son's and wept for very joy.

Chapter XIX

IN WHICH THE PROSPECTS FOR THE ARCHER FAMILY GROW BRIGHTER

THE city editor of the *Evening Wisconsin* looked distressed when a clergyman and a stout gentleman entered his sanctum.

"We have come to see you about a boy named Harry Archer," began the doctor, plunging, as usual, *in medias res.* "He wants to enter your mathematical contest; but, unfortunately, he can't sit up. Now, we want to know how he can manage to compete."

"I'm afraid he can't compete at all,"

answered the city editor, holding his pencil in the air and glancing anxiously at some copy before him.

"Is there no possible way of arranging it?" asked Father Trainer.

"No possible way."

"Pshaw!" cried Dr. Kendall, and he began to pull at his moustache.

There was a dreary pause, during which the city editor wished his visitors elsewhere. Suddenly Father Trainer, with a little cry of delight, made a dash for a bookshelf.

It was well filled with mathematical treatises.

"Oh, isn't this splendid! Why, it's a grand collection."

The city editor became suddenly interested.

"Please introduce me to that priest," he whispered to the doctor. And the city editor, reconsidering his wish, arose.

"Father Trainer, this is—"

"Father Trainer!" cried the editor. "Why, I am delighted to meet you. Your name is well known to me. I am so glad that you appreciate my collection. Now look here, for instance"—taking down a book—"here is a work published in 1746 by one of your Jesuit Fathers—"

Dr. Kendall took a chair and watched the two mathematicians bubbling and exulting over the book like a pair of children over a new toy.

Then the pair fell to discussing some *formulae*, evolved, I believe, by Father Trainer.

"I think I'll go, gentlemen," said the doctor, rising.

Neither mathematician took the least notice of him.

"Say!" he bawled as he stood at the door, "will you people make arrangements for that boy?"

Both mathematicians looked visibly annoyed.

"Oh, that's so!" exclaimed Father Trainer coming to himself. "What about the boy? I had forgotten all about him."

"Can he write lying down?"

"Yes," said the doctor.

"By the way, let me introduce you," put in Father Trainer. "Mr. Overbeck, this is my dear friend, Dr. Kendall."

"The great Dr. Kendall of Chicago?"

"Yes."

"When you two came in, I didn't know that I was entertaining angels unawares!" he exclaimed, giving the famous specialist a hearty handshake. "As regards that boy, if you think he's really good at mathematics and has a chance—"

"I answer for that," interrupted Father Trainer. "He's the best pupil I ever had."

"That's enough. I shall have a special apartment beside the reference room made ready for him with a lounge and shall engage a special conveyance to bring him there and back. It is a pleasure and an honor to me to have a chance to oblige such men as you."

Doctor Kendall contrived to get away in order to give a few hours to his book. He left with a smile of happiness; but his joy was as nothing to the joy of Father Trainer and Mr. Overbeck as they went into the discussion of the *formulae* already mentioned. Father Trainer had seldom met with a man who cared about discussing this particular discovery of his, and Mr. Overbeck seldom came into contact with people who made such discoveries.

On Wednesday morning an ambulance drove up to the public library. Harry was assisted out and helped to the elevator by Father Trainer and the good doctor. Thanks to the latter, the boy had enjoyed a good night's rest.

He was soon lying comfortably on a lounge in a private room, and sharp at nine he was locked in with paper and pen and a small printed slip containing seven propositions and eight problems in geometry. Four hours were allowed each of the eighty contestants. Harry finished the work in one hour and a half and took another half hour to assure himself that he had made no clerical errors. Having finished, he touched a bell at his side; the door was thrown open, and Father Trainer entered with one of the officials.

"Congratulations, Harry!" he exclaimed. "I see by your face that you've got it all. I knew you would as soon as I examined the questions. Here, take my arm. Oh! I am glad you came. After all, we have done the impossible. The other contestants, I am told, are still working away, and some of them, according to present indications, will not finish in a week."

Three days later, the result was announced.

Of the eighty contestants, only seventeen finished the work assigned. Harry's percentage was one hundred. He was easily first, the second in merit having made only eighty-one.

"There, mother!" cried the winner, presenting Mrs. Archer with the check for eighty dollars. "Now we shall be able to pay the interest on the mortgage."

"What mortgage?" asked Dr. Kendall, who was walking about the room in joyous nervousness.

Mrs. Archer explained.

"And have you enough money along with the eighty dollars to pay the entire interest?"

"We still lack twenty dollars, sir; but we shall doubtless be able to borrow that much."

"There is no need of borrowing," said the doctor, taking out his pocketbook [wallet]. "Allow me to pay for my board and lodgings in advance."

And so the difficulty about the mortgage was settled out of hand.

Chapter XX

*IN WHICH EVERYBODY IS HAPPY AND
THE CURTAIN FALLS*

THERE was great enthusiasm in the class of Poetry on February the second of the following year when Harry Archer, stout and hearty as in his best days, entered the room.

Mr. Keenan grasped his hand warmly.

"Welcome, Harry; we are all delighted to see you. If anything, you look better than at the opening of the school term in September."

"I think I am better, sir."

"We're going to have our baseball catcher again," said Claude.

"Oh, yes; you can count on me."

Harry took his seat and the lessons were presently resumed.

Since Harry's illness, many changes had taken place in his home. First of all, Dr. Kendall wanted a private secretary; in fact, he wanted an army of them. Alice was found to be most satisfactory; and this work, together with her music pupils and her own practice on the piano, kept that best of sisters busy and happy from Sunday morning till Saturday night.

In the next place, Frank Elmwood presented himself to Mrs. Archer on the very day that the interest on the mortgage was paid and said, "Mrs. Archer, I have come to ask you to do me a great favor."

"Certainly, Mr. Elmwood, if I can. Your constant kindness and attention to my boy since his illness have made me very deeply your debtor."

"Well, my family are about to leave Milwaukee to take up their residence in Philadelphia, where we came from originally. I am too much in love with Milwaukee to leave the place. Now couldn't you possibly allow me to live with you? I feel perfectly at home with you and Alice and Paul, while as for Harry—I like him and Claude Lightfoot above all the boys I have ever met, except Rob Collins. If you let me stay, you can settle about expenses according to your own judgment."

"You are doing me a favor, Frank. We have a spare room, and I've been praying for the right person to apply for it. You are just the one. How glad my poor Harry will be to have you near him!"

Within a week, Frank took up his lodgings with the Archers; and when he and Dr. Kendall and Alice and Paul and Harry assembled at the supper table, they formed the merriest assembly, I dare say, in that part of the city.

After supper, the neurologist would attack his book, Alice the piano, while Frank would accompany Harry to his room.

Then, while Harry lay upon his bed, Frank would read with enthusiasm favorite selections from his favorite poets, pausing, now and then, to point out some particular beauty whether of thought or of expression, to the listener. In this manner, the two made quite a satisfactory course in Longfellow, Tennyson, Wordsworth, Milton, and in certain plays of Shakespeare.

Elmwood was nothing if not literary. Harry caught his enthusiasm; and lo, the sleeping imagination was awakened! And in the silence of the night, Harry began to conceive and dwell upon beautiful thoughts and graceful turns of expression. During the day, when the young correspondent was pursuing his work, the boy would read again for himself what Frank had read to him on the preceding night—would read, would study, would ponder. Though meager in quantity, the matter thus studied was of the highest quality for a young student, and Harry was soon living in a new world, the world of the beautiful, of the ideal.

Hence, although he was forbidden to study, he succeeded during these three months of enforced leisure in making a good course in English reading.

It was early in January that more good fortune visited the Archers. Their shares in the silver mine suddenly rose from a nominal value to a high premium. There had been some mismanagement of the mine, and some dishonesty. The lawyer who had taken the case in hand in the interest of a number of shareholders succeeded in bringing affairs to rights; and, in consequence, Mrs. Archer was assured henceforth of a comfortable income. But this was not the end of their good fortune. As a recognition of the honor which Harry had brought upon his college by winning the prize in mathematics, Harry was awarded a scholarship at Milwaukee College.

*   *   *   *   *

Early in March, the third "reading of notes" took place in the college hall. To the surprise of his classmates, Harry received the medal in English Composition, with Claude in the second place.

"Boys," said Mr. Keenan, when his class had reassembled in their room, "I wish to read you the two papers which merited first and second prize in English. The first which I shall read is Claude Lightfoot's."

THE WHIP-POOR-WILL

When like a pall the shadows fall,
　And Hesper from his violet-curtained bed
　Uplifts his golden tressèd head,

And the evening dew from depths of blue
  Kisses to sleep the closing eyelids white
  Of the daisy, gentle flower of light,
We hear thy call like music fall,
  Thou herald of the night.

"Very pretty," commented Mr. Keenan. "Perhaps there are too many conceits for the length of the poem, but I esteem it for the promise with which it closes. Claude has the poetic ear and eye. Now I will read you Harry Archer's verses."

ODE TO EVENING

Hail, sister of the rosy Morn,
  Thy shadowy elf-locks drip
With showers of ambrosial dew,
  And thy sweet, rosy lip
Breathes forth the sweetness and the calm
Which are the tired spirit's balm.

Haste thee o'er the eastern mountains,
  Thy dim mystic shades encurling,
Where the sunlight sits embattled
  In the clouds, its banners furling—
  Its deep-crimson banners furling;
While around them float fantastic
Cloud-borne monsters of that main,
On whose deep-blue, endless plain
Phantom armies hold domain,
Ever grappling, ever waning,
Ever losing, ever gaining.

Come, and from each rustling fold
Of thy mantle green and gold

Shake out odors sweetly blent
By violets prim and roses lent,
And with gentle, dewy hand
Scatter sweets o'er all the land.

"Harry, I congratulate you sincerely. Although the verses are by no means perfect, and are here and there somewhat archaic, they give much promise. Contrast this with your first verses, which I read as an example of how verse is not to be written. The improvement is astonishing. For this improvement, I take no credit to myself at all. The best teacher you ever had was Seawell; and his one lesson was given in a short time indeed. I mean, when he tackled you at the goal line and sent you to bed for two months. I do not intend to preach a sermon, boys; but as I have heard that some student or students criticized the action of Divine Providence in dealing so severely with Harry, I simply wish to say that Harry's sickness, instead of turning out to be a misfortune, has proved to be a blessing."

"Yes, Claude," said Harry, returning Claude Lightfoot's enthusiastic grasp of congratulation with interest, as the two walked together through the yard, "everything has happened for the best. Even the loss of my poor father, which seemed so hard, has done me good in some ways. His death brought us poverty, and it has taken away some of my foolish pride and made me more in earnest."

"That's so," said Claude heartily.

"And then as regards that accident on the football field, it has taught me how kind and good the fellows are. And then as soon as I got sick, and just as I thought money matters were at their worst, everything began to go better. Secondly, my accident brought Dr. Kendall to our house—the best friend and the wisest doctor in the world. Then I had a chance to see how much nicer Father Trainer was than I thought him, and you know how much I thought of him. In the next place, that accident brought Frank Elmwood to our house, and to live with Frank as I have lived with him is almost a literary education in itself. Lastly, those three months at home forced me to read and awakened me to a new world."

"In a word," observed Claude, "that football game with the accident was the most fortunate thing that ever happened to you."

"I really believe it was."

"Halloa, Harry!" said Father Trainer. "Here you are again bigger and brighter than ever. So you and Claude carried off most of the honors—in English, too. I congratulate you both. As for you, Harry, when I see you here strong and active as ever with all trouble at home past and gone, I think with deep gratitude of those inspired words, "To them that love God, all things work together unto good."

THE END

If you have enjoyed this book, consider making your next selection from among the following . . .

The Guardian Angels 3.00
33 Doctors of the Church. *Fr. Rengers* 33.00
Angels and Devils. *Joan Carroll Cruz* 16.50
Eucharistic Miracles. *Joan Carroll Cruz* 16.50
The Incorruptibles. *Joan Carroll Cruz* 16.50
Padre Pio—The Stigmatist. *Fr. Charles Carty* 16.50
Ven. Francisco Marto of Fatima. *Cirrincione,* comp.. . . . 2.50
The Facts About Luther. *Msgr. P. O'Hare* 18.50
Little Catechism of the Curé of Ars. *St. John Vianney* . . 8.00
The Curé of Ars—Patron St. of Parish Priests. *O'Brien*. . 7.50
The Four Last Things: Death, Judgment, Hell, Heaven . . 9.00
Pope St. Pius X. *F. A. Forbes* 11.00
St. Alphonsus Liguori. *Frs. Miller & Aubin* 18.00
Confession of a Roman Catholic. *Paul Whitcomb* 2.50
The Catholic Church Has the Answer. *Paul Whitcomb* . . 2.50
The Sinner's Guide. *Ven. Louis of Granada* 15.00
True Devotion to Mary. *St. Louis De Montfort* 9.00
Life of St. Anthony Mary Claret. *Fanchón Royer* 16.50
Autobiography of St. Anthony Mary Claret 13.00
I Wait for You. *Sr. Josefa Menendez* 1.50
Words of Love. *Menendez, Betrone, Mary of the Trinity* . 8.00
Little Lives of the Great Saints. *John O'Kane Murray* . . 20.00
Prayer—The Key to Salvation. *Fr. Michael Müller*. 9.00
The Victories of the Martyrs. *St. Alphonsus Liguori* 13.50
Canons and Decrees of the Council of Trent. *Schroeder* . 16.50
Sermons of St. Alphonsus Liguori for Every Sunday . . . 18.50
A Catechism of Modernism. *Fr. J. B. Lemius* 7.50
Alexandrina—The Agony and the Glory. *Johnston* 7.00
Life of Blessed Margaret of Castello. *Fr. Bonniwell* 9.00
The Ways of Mental Prayer. *Dom Vitalis Lehodey* 16.50
The Story of the Church. *Johnson, Hannan, Dominica* . . 22.50
Hell Quizzes. *Radio Replies Press* 2.50
Purgatory Quizzes. *Radio Replies Press* 2.50
Virgin and Statue Worship Quizzes. *Radio Replies Press* . 2.50
Moments Divine before/Bl. Sacr. *Reuter* 10.00
Meditation Prayer on Mary Immaculate. *Padre Pio* 2.50
Little Book of the Work of Infinite Love. *de la Touche* . 3.50
Textual Concordance of/Holy Scriptures. *Williams. P.B.* . . 35.00
Douay-Rheims Bible. *Paperbound* 35.00
The Way of Divine Love. (pocket, unabr.). *Menendez* . . . 12.50
Mystical City of God—Abridged. *Ven. Mary of Agreda* . . 21.00

Prices subject to change.

Stories of Padre Pio. *Tangari*	9.00
Miraculous Images of Our Lady. *Joan Carroll Cruz*	21.50
Miraculous Images of Our Lord. *Cruz*	16.50
Brief Catechism for Adults. *Fr. Cogan*	12.50
Raised from the Dead. *Fr. Hebert*	18.50
Autobiography of St. Margaret Mary	7.50
Thoughts and Sayings of St. Margaret Mary	6.00
The Voice of the Saints. *Comp. by Francis Johnston*	8.00
The 12 Steps to Holiness and Salvation. *St. Alphonsus*	9.00
The Rosary and the Crisis of Faith. *Cirrincione/Nelson*	2.00
Sin and Its Consequences. *Cardinal Manning*	9.00
St. Francis of Paola. *Simi & Segreti*	9.00
Dialogue of St. Catherine of Siena. *Transl. Thorold*	12.50
Catholic Answer to Jehovah's Witnesses. *D'Angelo*	13.50
Twelve Promises of the Sacred Heart. (100 cards)	5.00
Life of St. Aloysius Gonzaga. *Fr. Meschler*	13.00
The Love of Mary. *D. Roberto*	9.00
Begone Satan. *Fr. Vogl*	4.00
The Prophets and Our Times. *Fr. R. G. Culleton*	15.00
St. Therese, The Little Flower. *John Beevers*	7.50
Mary, The Second Eve. *Cardinal Newman*	4.00
Devotion to Infant Jesus of Prague. *Booklet*	1.50
The Wonder of Guadalupe. *Francis Johnston*	9.00
Apologetics. *Msgr. Paul Glenn*	12.50
Baltimore Catechism No. 1	5.00
Baltimore Catechism No. 2	7.00
Baltimore Catechism No. 3	11.00
An Explanation of the Baltimore Catechism. *Kinkead*	18.00
Bible History. *Schuster*	16.50
Blessed Eucharist. *Fr. Mueller*	10.00
Catholic Catechism. *Fr. Faerber*	9.00
The Devil. *Fr. Delaporte*	8.50
Dogmatic Theology for the Laity. *Fr. Premm*	21.50
Evidence of Satan in the Modern World. *Cristiani*	14.00
Fifteen Promises of Mary. (100 cards)	5.00
Life of Anne Catherine Emmerich. 2 vols. *Schmoeger*	48.00
Life of the Blessed Virgin Mary. *Emmerich*	18.00
Prayer to St. Michael. (100 leaflets)	5.00
Prayerbook of Favorite Litanies. *Fr. Hebert*	12.50
Preparation for Death. (Abridged). *St. Alphonsus*	12.00
Purgatory Explained. *Schouppe*	16.50
Purgatory Explained. (pocket, unabr.). *Schouppe*	12.00
Spiritual Conferences. *Tauler*	15.00
Trustful Surrender to Divine Providence. *Bl. Claude*	7.00

Prices subject to change.

Forty Dreams of St. John Bosco. *Bosco* 15.00
Blessed Miguel Pro. *Ball* 7.50
Soul Sanctified. *Anonymous* 12.00
Wife, Mother and Mystic. *Bessieres* 10.00
The Agony of Jesus. *Padre Pio* 3.00
Catholic Home Schooling. *Mary Kay Clark* 21.00
The Cath. Religion—Illus. & Expl. *Msgr. Burbach* 12.50
Wonders of the Holy Name. *Fr. O'Sullivan* 2.50
How Christ Said the First Mass. *Fr. Meagher*. 21.00
Too Busy for God? Think Again! *D'Angelo* 7.00
St. Bernadette Soubirous. *Trochu*. 21.00
Pope Pius VII. *Anderson*. 16.50
Life Everlasting. *Garrigou-Lagrange* 16.50
Confession Quizzes. *Radio Replies Press*. 2.50
St. Philip Neri. *Fr. V. J. Matthews*. 7.50
St. Louise de Marillac. *Sr. Vincent Regnault*. 7.50
The Old World and America. *Rev. Philip Furlong* 21.00
Prophecy for Today. *Edward Connor* 7.50
Bethlehem. *Fr. Faber*. 20.00
The Book of Infinite Love. *Mother de la Touche* 7.50
The Church Teaches. *Church Documents* 18.00
Conversation with Christ. *Peter T. Rohrbach* 12.50
Purgatory and Heaven. *J. P. Arendzen* 6.00
Liberalism Is a Sin. *Sarda y Salvany* 9.00
Spiritual Legacy/Sr. Mary of Trinity. *van den Broek*. . . . 13.00
The Creator and the Creature. *Fr. Frederick Faber* 17.50
Radio Replies. 3 Vols. *Frs. Rumble and Carty* 48.00
Convert's Catechism of Catholic Doctrine. *Geiermann*. . . 5.00
Incarnation, Birth, Infancy of Jesus Christ. *Liguori* 13.50
Light and Peace. *Fr. R. P. Quadrupani* 8.00
Dogmatic Canons & Decrees of Trent, Vat. I 11.00
The Evolution Hoax Exposed. *A. N. Field*. 9.00
The Priest, the Man of God. *St. Joseph Cafasso* 16.00
Christ Denied. *Fr. Paul Wickens* 3.50
New Regulations on Indulgences. *Fr. Winfrid Herbst* . . . 3.00
A Tour of the Summa. *Msgr. Paul Glenn* 22.50
Spiritual Conferences. *Fr. Frederick Faber* 18.00
Bible Quizzes. *Radio Replies Press* 2.50
Marriage Quizzes. *Radio Replies Press* 2.50
True Church Quizzes. *Radio Replies Press*. 2.50
Mary, Mother of the Church. *Church Documents* 5.00
The Sacred Heart and the Priesthood. *de la Touche* 10.00
Blessed Sacrament. *Fr. Faber*. 20.00
Revelations of St. Bridget. *St. Bridget of Sweden* 4.50

Prices subject to change.

Story of a Soul. *St. Therese of Lisieux* 9.00
Catholic Dictionary. *Attwater* 24.00
Catholic Children's Treasure Box Books 1-10 . . . . 50.00
Prayers and Heavenly Promises. *Cruz* 6.00
Magnificent Prayers. *St. Bridget of Sweden* 2.00
The Happiness of Heaven. *Fr. J. Boudreau* 10.00
The Holy Eucharist—Our All. *Fr. Lucas Etlin* 3.00
The Glories of Mary. *St. Alphonsus Liguori* 21.00
The Curé D'Ars. *Abbé Francis Trochu* 24.00
Humility of Heart. *Fr. Cajetan da Bergamo* 9.00
Love, Peace and Joy. (St. Gertrude). *Prévot* 8.00
Passion of Jesus & Its Hidden Meaning. *Groenings* 15.00
Mother of God & Her Glorious Feasts. *Fr. O'Laverty* . . . 15.00
Song of Songs—A Mystical Exposition. *Fr. Arintero* . . . 21.50
Love and Service of God, Infinite Love. *de la Touche* . . 15.00
Life & Work of Mother Louise Marg. *Fr. O'Connell* . . . 15.00
Martyrs of the Coliseum. *O'Reilly* 21.00
Rhine Flows into the Tiber. *Fr. Wiltgen* 16.50
What Catholics Believe. *Fr. Lawrence Lovasik* 6.00
Who Is Therese Neumann? *Fr. Charles Carty* 3.50
Summa of the Christian Life. 3 Vols. *Granada* 43.00
St. Francis of Paola. *Simi and Segreti* 9.00
The Rosary in Action. *John Johnson* 12.00
St. Dominic. *Sr. Mary Jean Dorcy* 13.50
Is It a Saint's Name? *Fr. William Dunne* 3.00
St. Martin de Porres. *Giuliana Cavallini* 15.00
Douay-Rheims New Testament. *Paperbound* 16.50
St. Catherine of Siena. *Alice Curtayne* 16.50
Blessed Virgin Mary. *Liguori* 7.50
Chats With Converts. *Fr. M. D. Forrest* 13.50
The Stigmata and Modern Science. *Fr. Charles Carty* . . . 2.50
St. Gertrude the Great 2.50
Thirty Favorite Novenas 1.50
Brief Life of Christ. *Fr. Rumble* 3.50
Catechism of Mental Prayer. *Msgr. Simler* 3.00
On Freemasonry. *Pope Leo XIII* 2.50
Thoughts of the Curé D'Ars. *St. John Vianney* 3.00
Incredible Creed of Jehovah Witnesses. *Fr. Rumble* 3.00
St. Pius V—His Life, Times, Miracles. *Anderson* 7.00
St. Dominic's Family. *Sr. Mary Jean Dorcy* 27.50
St. Rose of Lima. *Sr. Alphonsus* 16.50
Latin Grammar. *Scanlon & Scanlon* 18.00
Second Latin. *Scanlon & Scanlon* 16.50
St. Joseph of Copertino. *Pastrovicchi* 8.00

Prices subject to change.

Holy Eucharist—Our All. *Fr. Lukas Etlin, O.S.B.*. 3.00
Glories of Divine Grace. *Fr. Scheeben* 18.00
Saint Michael and the Angels. *Approved Sources*. 9.00
Dolorous Passion of Our Lord. *Anne C. Emmerich*. 18.00
Our Lady of Fatima's Peace Plan from Heaven. *Booklet* . 1.00
Three Ways of the Spiritual Life. *Garrigou-Lagrange* . . . 7.00
Mystical Evolution. 2 Vols. *Fr. Arintero, O.P.*. 42.00
St. Catherine Labouré of the Mirac. Medal. *Fr. Dirvin* . . 16.50
Manual of Practical Devotion to St. Joseph. *Patrignani*. . 17.50
The Active Catholic. *Fr. Palau*. 9.00
Ven. Jacinta Marto of Fatima. *Cirrincione* 3.00
Reign of Christ the King. *Davies* 2.00
St. Teresa of Avila. *William Thomas Walsh* 24.00
Isabella of Spain—The Last Crusader. *Wm. T. Walsh* . . . 24.00
Characters of the Inquisition. *Wm. T. Walsh*. 16.50
Blood-Drenched Altars—Cath. Comment. Hist. Mexico . . 21.50
Self-Abandonment to Divine Providence. *de Caussade* . . 22.50
Way of the Cross. *Liguorian* 1.50
Way of the Cross. *Franciscan* 1.50
Modern Saints—Their Lives & Faces, Bk. 1. *Ann Ball* . . 21.00
Modern Saints—Their Lives & Faces, Bk. 2. *Ann Ball* . . 23.00
Divine Favors Granted to St. Joseph. *Pere Binet* 7.50
St. Joseph Cafasso—Priest of the Gallows. *St. J. Bosco* . 6.00
Catechism of the Council of Trent. *McHugh/Callan* 27.50
Why Squander Illness? *Frs. Rumble & Carty* 4.00
Fatima—The Great Sign. *Francis Johnston* 12.00
Heliotropium—Conformity of Human Will to Divine . . . 15.00
Charity for the Suffering Souls. *Fr. John Nageleisen* . . . 18.00
Devotion to the Sacred Heart of Jesus. *Verheylezoon* . . . 16.50
Sermons on Prayer. *St. Francis de Sales* 7.00
Sermons on Our Lady. *St. Francis de Sales* 15.00
Sermons for Lent. *St. Francis de Sales*. 15.00
Fundamentals of Catholic Dogma. *Ott* 27.50
Litany of the Blessed Virgin Mary. (100 cards) 5.00
Who Is Padre Pio? *Radio Replies Press* 3.00
Child's Bible History. *Knecht*. 7.00
St. Anthony—The Wonder Worker of Padua. *Stoddard* . . 7.00
The Precious Blood. *Fr. Faber* 16.50
The Holy Shroud & Four Visions. *Fr. O'Connell* 3.50
Clean Love in Courtship. *Fr. Lawrence Lovasik* 4.50
The Secret of the Rosary. *St. Louis De Montfort* 5.00

At your Bookdealer or direct from the Publisher.
Toll Free 1-800-437-5876   ***www.tanbooks.com***

Prices subject to change.

Catholic Books for Young People

Catholic Children's Treasure Box Books 1-10 (Ages 3-8+) . . 50.00
Catholic Children's Treasure Box Books 11-20 (Ages 3-8+) . . 50.00
My Confession Book. *Sr. M. A. Welters*. (Ages 6-10) 2.00
My See and Pray Missal. *Sr. J. Therese*. (Ages 4-8) 2.00
Set of 20 Saints' Lives by Mary Fabyan Windeatt. 160.00
Children of Fatima. *Windeatt*. (Ages 10 & up) 11.00
Curé of Ars. *Windeatt*. (Ages 10 & up) 13.00
Little Flower. *Windeatt*. (Ages 10 & up) 11.00
Patron St./First Communicants. *Windeatt*. (Ages 10 & up) . . . 8.00
Miraculous Medal. *Windeatt*. (Ages 10 & up) 9.00
St. Thomas Aquinas. *Windeatt*. (Ages 10 & up) 8.00
St. Catherine of Siena. *Windeatt*. (Ages 10 & up) 7.00
St. Rose of Lima. *Windeatt*. (Ages 10 & up) 10.00
St. Benedict. *Windeatt*. (Ages 10 & up) 11.00
St. Louis De Montfort. *Windeatt*. (Ages 10 & up) 13.00
Saint Hyacinth of Poland. *Windeatt*. (Ages 10 & up) 13.00
Saint Martin de Porres. *Windeatt*. (Ages 10 & up) 10.00
Pauline Jaricot. *Windeatt*. (Ages 10 & up) 15.00
St. Paul the Apostle. *Windeatt*. (Ages 10 & up) 15.00
King David and His Songs. *Windeatt*. (Ages 10 & up) 11.00
St. Francis Solano. *Windeatt*. (Ages 10 & up) 14.00
St. John Masias. *Windeatt*. (Ages 10 & up) 11.00
Blessed Marie of New France. *Windeatt*. (Ages 10 & up) . . . 11.00
St. Margaret Mary. *Windeatt*. (Ages 10 & up) 14.00
St. Dominic. *Windeatt*. (Ages 10 & up) 11.00
Anne—Life/Ven. Anne de Guigne (1911-1922). *Benedictine Nun*. 7.00
Under Angel Wings—True Story/Young Girl & Guardian Angel. 9.00
Pope St. Pius X. *F. A. Forbes*. 11.00
Child's Bible History. *M. Rev. F. J. Knecht*. 7.00
Forty Dreams of St. John Bosco. *St. John Bosco* 15.00
Blessed Miguel Pro—20th Century Mexican Martyr. *Ann Ball* 7.50
Story of a Soul. *St. Therese*. 9.00
The Guardian Angels. 3.00
St. Maria Goretti—In Garments All Red. *Fr. G. Poage*. 7.00
The Curé of Ars—Patron Saint of Parish Priests. *Fr. O'Brien*. 7.50
St. Maximilian Kolbe—Knight of the Immaculata. *Fr. J. J. Smith*. 7.00
Life of Blessed Margaret of Castello. *Bonniwell*. 9.00
Story/Church—Her Founding/Mission/Progress. (7th-12th Grades) 22.50
Bible History. *Johnson, Hannan & Dominica*. (Grades 6-9+) . 24.00
Bible History Workbook (to accompany above). *Ignatz*. 21.00
Set: Bible History Text & Workbook. 36.00

Prices subject to change.

St. Teresa of Avila. *F. A. Forbes*. (Youth–Adult) 7.00
St. Ignatius Loyola. *F. A. Forbes*. (Youth–Adult) 7.00
St. Athanasius. *F. A. Forbes*. (Youth–Adult) 7.00
St. Vincent de Paul. *F. A. Forbes*. (Youth–Adult) 7.00
St. Catherine of Siena. *F. A. Forbes*. (Youth–Adult) 7.00
St. John Bosco—Friend of Youth. *F. A. Forbes*. (Youth–Adult) 9.00
St. Monica. *F. A. Forbes*. (Youth–Adult) 7.00
Set of 7 Saints' Lives above by F. A. Forbes. ($51.00 value) 39.00
Set of 24 Catholic Story Coloring Books. *Windeatt & Harmon* 72.00
Our Lady of Fatima Catholic Story Coloring Book. 4.50
Our Lady of Lourdes Catholic Story Coloring Book. 4.50
Our Lady of Guadalupe Catholic Story Coloring Book. 4.50
Our Lady of the Miraculous Medal Catholic Story Coloring Bk. 4.50
Our Lady of La Salette Catholic Story Coloring Book. 4.50
Our Lady of Knock Catholic Story Coloring Book. 4.50
Our Lady of Beauraing Catholic Story Coloring Book. 4.50
Our Lady of Banneux Catholic Story Coloring Book. 4.50
Our Lady of Pontmain Catholic Story Coloring Book. 4.50
Our Lady of Pellevoisin Catholic Story Coloring Book. 4.50
St. Joan of Arc Catholic Story Coloring Book. 4.50
St. Francis of Assisi Catholic Story Coloring Book. 4.50
St. Anthony of Padua Catholic Story Coloring Book. 4.50
St. Dominic Savio Catholic Story Coloring Book. 4.50
St. Pius X Catholic Story Coloring Book. 4.50
St. Teresa of Avila Catholic Story Coloring Book. 4.50
St. Philomena Catholic Story Coloring Book. 4.50
St. Maria Goretti Catholic Story Coloring Book. 4.50
St. Frances Cabrini Catholic Story Coloring Book. 4.50
St. Christopher Catholic Story Coloring Book. 4.50
St. Meinrad Catholic Story Coloring Book. 4.50
Bl. Kateri Tekakwitha Catholic Story Coloring Book. 4.50
The Rosary Catholic Story Coloring Book. 4.50
The Brown Scapular Catholic Story Coloring Book. 4.50
Christ the King—Lord of History. *Anne Carroll*. (H. S. Text). 24.00
Christ the King, Lord of History Workbook. *Mooney*.. . . . . . 21.00
Set: Christ the King Text and Workbook. 36.00
Christ and the Americas. *Anne Carroll*. (High School Text). . 24.00
Old World and America. *Bishop Furlong*. (Grades 5-8). 21.00
Old World and America Answer Key. *McDevitt*. 10.00
Our Pioneers and Patriots. *Bishop Furlong*. (Grades 5-8). . . . 24.00
Our Pioneers and Patriots Answer Key. *McDevitt*. (Grades 5-8). 10.00

At your Bookdealer or direct from the Publisher.
Toll Free 1-800-437-5876   *www.tanbooks.com*

Prices subject to change.

From the cover of Tom Playfair . . .

TOM PLAYFAIR is one of "Fr. Finn's Famous Three"—**Tom Playfair**, **Percy Wynn** and **Harry Dee**. These were the most popular of Fr. Finn's 27 Catholic novels for young people. Resembling a Catholic version of Charles Dickens' stories, or even *The Hardy Boys*, these books were read by hundreds of thousands of young people in the late 19th and early-to-mid 20th century. Their quaint turn-of-the-century language is part of the charm of the stories and of Fr. Finn's own brand of humor. After young readers (or hearers) have "gotten into" his style, they find it hilarious! But besides being fun, the stories have a moral: Tom Playfair is an unruly little boy when he is sent to St. Maure's boarding school, but he develops into a good Catholic young man and leader—without ever losing his high spirits. (All 3 books feature Tom Playfair.)

But what about today's young people?

We were given great encouragement to reprint these books by the experience of a teaching Sister who reads all 3 books each year to her 5th and 6th graders—with very gratifying results. Sister says she has seen drastic changes in students after hearing Fr. Finn's stories—marked improvement in behavior, motivation *and character*, especially in boys. Though both boys and girls enjoy the books immensely, she says, "It's the boys that absolutely love them. It's a hero worship thing." And parents ask: "Who's this Tom Playfair?—because that's all the kids talk about at the dinner table on Monday nights."

Grade level: 5th-8th (and older!)

Tom Playfair was "the most successful book for Catholic boys and girls ever published in the English language." —Benziger Brothers Publishers

Perfect for reading aloud at home or at school! Great for book reports! Include an "About the Author."

TOM PLAYFAIR

The story opens with 10-year-old Tom Playfair being quite a handful for his well-meaning but soft-hearted aunt. (Tom's mother has died.) Mr. Playfair decides to ship his son off to St. Maure's boarding school—an all-boys academy run by Jesuits—to shape him up, as well as to help him make a good preparation for his upcoming First Communion. Tom's adventures are just about to begin. Life at St. Maure's will not be dull!

PERCY WYNN

In this volume, Tom Playfair meets a new boy just arriving at St. Maure's. Percy Wynn has grown up in a family of 10 girls and only 1 boy—himself! His manners are formal, he talks like a book, and he has never played baseball or gone skating, boating, fishing, or even swimming! Yet he has brains, courage and high Catholic ideals. Tom and his buddies at St. Maure's befriend Percy and have a great time as they all work at turning Percy into an all-American Catholic boy.

HARRY DEE

Young Harry Dee arrives at St. Maure's thin and pale from his painful experiences involving the murder of his rich uncle. In this last book of the three, Tom and Percy help Harry recover from his early trauma—which involves solving "the mystery of Tower Hill Mansion." After many wild experiences, the three boys graduate from St. Maure's and head toward the life work to which God is calling each of them as young men.

Fr. Francis J. Finn, S.J. with *Dial* staff at St. Mary's College, St. Mary's, Kansas, 1894-1895.

ABOUT THE AUTHOR

Fr. Francis J. Finn, S.J.
1859-1928

THE son of Irish immigrant parents, Francis J. Finn, S.J. was born on October 4, 1859 in St. Louis, Missouri; there he grew up, attending parochial schools. As a boy, Francis was deeply impressed with Cardinal Wiseman's famous novel of the early Christian martyrs, *Fabiola*. After that, religion really began to mean something to him.

Eleven-year-old Francis was a voracious reader; he read the works of Charles Dickens, devouring *Nicholas Nickleby* and *The Pickwick Papers*. From his First Communion at age 12, Francis began to desire to become a Jesuit priest; but then his fervor cooled, his grades dropped, and his vocation might have been lost except for Fr. Charles Coppens. Fr. Coppens urged Francis to apply himself to his Latin, to improve it by using an all-Latin prayerbook, and to read good Catholic books. Fr. Finn credited the saving of his vocation to this advice and to his membership in the Sodality of Our Lady.

Francis began his Jesuit novitiate and seminary studies on March 24, 1879. As a young Jesuit scholastic, he suffered from repeated bouts of sickness. He would be sent home to recover, would return in robust health, then would come down with another ailment. Normally this would have been seen as a sign that he did not have a vocation, yet his superiors kept him on. Fr. Finn commented, "God often uses instruments most unfit to do His work."

During his seminary days Mr. Finn was assigned as prefect of St. Mary's boarding school or "college" in St. Mary's, Kansas (which became the fictional "St. Maure's"). There he learned—often the hard way—how to teach and discipline boys.

ABOUT THE AUTHOR

One afternoon while supervising a class who were busy writing a composition, Mr. Finn thought of how they represented to him the typical American Catholic boy. With nothing else to do, he took up pencil and paper. "Why not write about such boys as are before me?" he asked himself. In no time at all he had dashed off the first chapter of *Tom Playfair*. When he read it aloud to the class, they loved it! Of course they wanted more.

Francis was finally ordained to the priesthood around 1891. This was the year that *Tom Playfair* was published. Fr. Finn's publisher, Benziger Brothers, was to call *Tom Playfair* "the most successful book for boys and girls ever published in the English language." Fr. Finn would write 27 books in all, which would be translated into as many as ten languages, and even into Braille.

Fr. Finn spent many years of his priestly life at St. Xavier's in Cinncinati. There he was well loved, and it is said that wherever he went—if he took a taxi, ate at a restaurant, attended a baseball game—people would not take his money for their services, but instead would press money into his hand for his many charities. Children especially loved him. It is said that at his death in 1928, children by the thousands turned out to mourn their departed friend.

It was Fr. Finn's lifelong conviction that "One of the greatest things in the world is to get the right book into the hands of the right boy or girl. No one can indulge in reading to any extent without being largely influenced for better or worse."

According to the *American Catholic Who's Who*, Fr. Finn is "universally acknowledged the foremost Catholic writer of fiction for young people."

Photo of Fr. Finn courtesy of Midwest Jesuit Archives, St. Louis, Missouri. Biographical sketch from various sources, including an article in *Crusade* magazine which was based on Fr. Finn's memoirs as edited and published by Fr. Daniel A. Lord, S.J., in a book entitled *Fr. Finn, S.J.*